Unhappy Appy

★★★★★

Winnie
The HORSE GENTLER

5 Unhappy Appy

Dandi Daley Mackall

TYNDALE KIDS

Tyndale House Publishers, Inc.
Wheaton, Illinois

Visit the exciting Web site for kids at www.cool2read.com and the Winnie the Horse Gentler Web site at www.winniethehorsegentler.com

You can contact Dandi Daley Mackall through her Web site at www.dandibooks.com

Interior horse chart given by permission, Arabian Horse Registry of America®. www.theregistry.org

Designed by Beth Sparkman

Edited by Ramona Cramer Tucker

Scripture quotations are taken from the *Holy Bible*, New Living Translation, copyright © 1996. Used by permission of Tyndale House Publishers, Inc., Wheaton, Illinois 60189. All rights reserved.

ISBN 0-8423-5546-4, mass paper

Printed in the United States of America

08 07 06 05 04 03
7   6   5   4   3   2   1

*To my future
son-in-law, Dave,
who is my
daughter Jen's
Catman*

Towaco, no!" I jumped from the paddock fence and raced to the pasture.

The grumpy Appaloosa ignored me. Ears flat back, teeth bared, he wheeled on Nickers, my white Arabian.

All Nickers had done was rest her head on the Appy's back. I'd seen them do it a dozen times. But this time Towaco wanted no part of it.

"Nickers, run!" I shouted, trying to get to them. I stumbled over a clump of slimy brown leaves.

My horse nickered, the friendliest sound in the world. She lifted her head to greet me.

"Nickers, look out!"

Towaco's head shot forward like a snapping turtle's.

I heard a *crunch* as the Appy's teeth closed around Nickers' horseflesh.

Nickers let out a squeal and skidded back.

I raced up to her. "Nickers, are you all right?" I ran my hand down her neck and chest until I felt the teeth marks. Towaco had caught skin high on Nickers' chest. Two tiny patches of hair were missing, but there wasn't any blood.

I hugged my horse, feeling the pain myself, as if Towaco had bitten *me* in the chest. "Don't feel bad, girl," I murmured, pressing my cheek against her neck, feeling the early winter fuzz. "I know. You were just being a buddy."

I glared at Towaco. He stood a few yards off, head lowered, but not grazing.

A picture of Nickers and Towaco a couple of months earlier flashed into my head. Like it or not, I have a photographic memory. It would be great if I could choose the pictures my brain takes, but I can't. This photo came in full-blown color, showing the same two horses, but with Nickers as the bad guy, ready to kick a frightened Towaco.

Back in August, Victoria Hawkins had brought me her Appaloosa, the first problem horse for my new business as Winnie the Horse

Gentler. Dad had sold our ranch in Wyoming after Mom died. Then he moved my sister, Lizzy, and me around for two years until we ended up here, in the last house in Ashland, Ohio, on the very edge of town. At first, I hadn't expected to stay in Ohio any longer than we'd lived in the *I* states—Illinois, Indiana, and Iowa.

But a lot had happened since then. I'd ended up with my own horse, the most beautiful white Arabian in the whole world. People around here were pretty amazed that a kid like me, who looks even younger than twelve because she's so short, could tame a horse everybody called Wild Thing. So I got a reputation like my mom had in Wyoming for gentling horses instead of breaking them. Mom taught me how to pay attention to the little details of a horse—how he holds his tail, twitches his withers, blinks his eyes, communicates.

Victoria Hawkins, who answers to "Hawk" when she's not with our other classmates, had talked her mother into letting me work with her Appaloosa. The gelding had picked up some bad habits at Spidells' Stable-Mart, a fancy stable across town, and I knew all he needed was pasture time. But the minute I'd turned Towaco out with Nickers, Nickers had wheeled around and kicked.

Remembering, seeing that mind picture of Towaco on the receiving end of mean, kept me from getting too angry at him now. "Come here, Towaco!" I called. "Let's all make up, huh?"

Towaco didn't stir, didn't even twitch an ear. The Appy had been acting weird for over a week, ready to fight one minute and the next minute acting like he was too tired to come in for dinner.

"Hey, Winnie!" Lizzy, her brown hair pulled up in a perfect ponytail, raced by on the other side of the fence. People say my sister and I look alike, but Lizzy, who's a year younger than me, is two inches taller. She doesn't have my freckles. And even though our hair's the same color, hers never looks like she just stepped out of a tornado. Without even trying, Lizzy was already the most popular girl in her sixth-grade class.

Behind Lizzy ran a girl about her size, with a short, blonde ponytail. The kid wore jeans and a navy sweatshirt like my sister's.

"This is Geri!" Lizzy shouted.

So that was Geri. Lately, every other word that came from my sister's mouth—and that was

4

a *lot* of words—was *Geri*. If they weren't off somewhere together, they were talking on the phone.

Geri waved. "You're Lizzy's *big* sister?" she shouted.

I nodded.

Lizzy didn't stop. "Geri thinks she heard a peeper! Frog!"

If Geri loved frogs like my sister loved lizards, small wonder they'd ended up best friends. Back in Wyoming, Lizzy had her own lizard farm. Kids from school took field trips just to see her collection.

Nickers rubbed her soft muzzle into my neck. I think Towaco had hurt her feelings more than anything. It was like she'd lost her best horse friend.

I blew gently into her nostrils. It was an old Indian trick my mom had taught me, a sign of friendship horses exchange among themselves. Nickers snorted back.

"I know just how you feel." Something had been kicking up inside me, and I couldn't explain it. I've always considered horses my best friends. People are too hard to figure out. But lately, I'd had a longing for a human best friend.

5

Maybe it was because Lizzy was gone so much with Geri now, or because it seemed like everybody else in middle school fell into best friends.

Or maybe it was one more way of missing my mom, who had been my best friend right up to the day she died.

Whatever it was, I'd been thinking about it all week. Hawk was the closest thing I had to a best friend. When we weren't in school, we had fun riding horses together. We'd even ridden in a circus once.

At school it was a different story. Middle-school kids aren't that different from horses in the wild, splitting off into "herds" and jockeying for position in their groups. Hawk's herd was the popular group, and I didn't fit in. It had taken some time, but things had gotten better. At least Hawk wasn't afraid to say hello to me at school. Most of the time, she acted like my friend.

But for the past week or two, Hawk had been neglecting Towaco *and* me. Every day she came up with a different excuse why she couldn't ride with me.

Now, finally, Hawk had agreed to a Saturday ride. I might have known today would be the day her horse would act up.

"Towaco?" I tried calling him again, but he acted deaf.

I headed toward the barn for oats to coax the Appy in. Nickers trailed after me, nudging my back to speed me up. A late-fall wetness hung in the morning air under a gray sky that made it feel like dusk.

When we stepped into the paddock, a handful of sparrows shot out of the barn. I squinted to see inside. "Hawk?"

Something rustled in the doorway, and out came four cats. One was my barn cat, Nelson, the sweetest little black kitty, with one white paw he manages to keep clean, even on muddy days. I recognized the two orange tabby cats as Moggie and Wilhemina, part of Catman's brood.

"Hey, Catman!" I called, picking up Nelson and setting him on Nickers' back. My kitty curled up and purred, rocking as Nickers walked smoothly into the barn.

Catman Coolidge nodded as Nickers passed him. "Far out, man." Catman should have been born in the 60s, when he wouldn't have been the only hippie in town. I'd gotten used to his striped bell-bottoms, tie-dyed shirts, long, wavy

7

blond hair, and leather thong sandals, which he wore even on chilly days like this one.

"Like, coming or going?" Catman asked. Half a dozen more cats crept in from the pasture, the yard, the south field, all intent on getting Catman's attention. Lizzy calls him the Pied Piper of Cats.

"Hawk's supposed to come over and ride with me," I said, following Nickers into the barn.

"Groovy." Catman knew Hawk had been acting weird toward me. He has a quiet way of making me tell him things I never planned to tell anybody.

It took a minute for my eyes to adjust to the dark barn. I love our barn. Actually it's owned by Pat Haven, my substitute science teacher and my boss at Pat's Pets. The gray barn slats let in just enough light to send streaks of hay dust dancing through the row of stalls. And the whole barn smells like horse and hay and home.

I turned to see if Towaco had followed us, but he hadn't. "Maybe not so groovy—not if I can't get Towaco to come around. That Appy has been acting as strange as Hawk, Catman. He bit Nickers."

"Downer." Catman stretched his long neck to

gaze out at the Appaloosa. "Dude looks sad, man. Unhappy Appy."

It was exactly what I'd been thinking, that the only thing wrong with Towaco was that he was sad. I think he missed Hawk. Even when Hawk did stop by to see her horse, she was sharp and impatient with him. "Maybe a great ride through the fields with Nickers and me will fix Towaco *and* Hawk."

I fetched a plastic bucket and dipped some oats into it. Nickers nickered at me, expecting at least a handful. I gave her two.

"Catman, I thought you and Barker would be at Pat's Pets all morning."

Eddy Barker is my age and just about the nicest person I know. He and Catman are best friends. Barker loves dogs the way I love horses and Catman loves cats. The three of us make up the Pet Help Line staff at Pat's Pets, answering e-mails people send in about their problem pets.

Catman let Nelson curl around his neck. The tip of Nelson's black tail swayed in front of Catman's nose. "Barker's in Texas. The annual Barker Thanksgiving reunion."

"Lucky Barker." I didn't just mean because he'd be missing a couple days of school. Barker has the greatest family, and I was trying to imagine what a reunion full of Barkers would be like. Mr. and Mrs. Barker teach African-American studies, computer science, poetry, and classy stuff at Ashland University. "What are they doing with the dogs?" Barker had trained a dog for each of his five brothers.

"Traveling with," Catman answered. "Can you dig it?"

I tried to imagine the Barker bus en route with five dogs, six kids, two parents, and one grandmother.

"I better saddle Towaco before Hawk gets here, Catman. I don't want to give her an excuse to back out." Tossing him a leadrope, I added, "Follow me, and keep that rope behind your back."

I carried the bucket of oats to the pasture. Towaco was standing in the same spot, his head low, ears lopped to the sides. He's a perfect, blanket-patterned Appy, dark brown with a solid white blanket over his rump and hips, brown spots scattered over the blanket.

"Mmmm. Look what I've got, Towaco. Oats!" I shook the bucket and let the grain swish against the sides.

The Appy's ears flicked, but he didn't come.

"Bummer," Catman muttered from a few feet away.

Nickers came trotting up behind me.

"You don't want Nickers to get it all, do you?" I asked, walking up to the Appaloosa.

Nickers nuzzled over my shoulder, around my arm, trying to stick her nose into the bucket.

Towaco let me walk up to him but didn't even glance at the bucket. Something was really wrong. Horses are curious, especially about food. I held a handful of oats a foot from his nose, but he wouldn't take a step toward me. Finally I gave up and moved the oats under his lips. He took my handful of grain, but didn't ask for more.

Nickers stuck her head under my arm and into the bucket, greedily lipping up the grain. Towaco didn't blink. He let out a horse sigh and dropped his head even lower.

"Carrots!" I cried, remembering how much the Appaloosa loved the carrots Hawk used to bring him. I shoved the bucket at Catman. "See if you can do anything with Towaco. I'll be right back."

I ran through the pasture toward the house,

calling back to Catman, "If Hawk comes, do whatever it takes! But don't let her leave!"

I treaded carefully through our yard, jumping over lawn-mower parts, broken vacuum cleaners, dissected toasters, and other small appliances—my dad's "works-in-progress."

People call Dad "Odd Job Willis." He can fix anything they bring him, unless he gets distracted by his inventions. Dad thinks of himself as Inventor Willis, which is a long ways from what he was in Wyoming—Mr. Jack Willis, boss of an insurance company.

I leaped over a wad of coiled wires to our front step and nearly landed on a long, skinny, black shoe. It wasn't like any shoe I'd ever seen. A rectangular bump on the tip of the toe looked like a switch. I picked up the shoe and flipped the switch. Out came a miniature garden shovel. When I did the same thing to the other shoe, a tiny spade popped out.

Carrying the shoes inside with me, I called out, "Hey, Dad! What's with the shoes?" I figured they must be one of his latest inventions. And I hoped he didn't expect *me* to wear them.

I crossed the living room to the kitchen. "Dad, I—!"

Dad was on his knees, wrestling with a large, black umbrella. But he wasn't alone. *She* was with him. Madeline. Madeline Edison, fellow inventor. Dad met her at the Invention Convention in Chicago and discovered she lived in Loudonville, only a few miles from us. Lucky us.

I couldn't take my eyes off them. What could my father be thinking, bringing a strange woman into our very own kitchen! I felt my ears go back, like Towaco's. If they'd been horses, I'd have bitten them!

2

*N*either Dad nor *the woman* turned from the black umbrella on the kitchen floor. It struck me that redheaded Madeline Edison was kind of umbrella-shaped herself, if the umbrella's red and closed. She's tall, thin, and pointy. She wore shiny black slacks and a red sweater and seemed totally fascinated with Dad's umbrella.

I cleared my throat and opened the fridge.

"Winnie?" Dad asked, sounding surprised to find *me* in the kitchen.

"Carrots," I mumbled, my head deep in the fridge.

"You remember Ms. Edison, don't you?" he asked.

Like I could forget her. I'd met her right after Dad got back from the Invention Convention. I suspected Dad had seen her a couple of times since then. I'd answered the phone once when she called. But this was the first time, as far as I knew, that she'd actually set foot in our house.

Foot! I realized I was still holding the shoes, which, judging by Madeline's stocking feet, must have been hers.

Note to self: Let sleeping shoes lie.

Maybe I could sneak the shoes back outside before they noticed . . .

"Hello, Winnie," Madeline said. "Like my shoes?"

Before I could answer that I hated her shoes, had no idea how they'd gotten into my hands, she was by my side, staring down at me from her great height. "They're my garden shoes," she explained. "If I don't feel like bending over, I wear these and let my feet do the digging."

I handed them to her and tried not to look like I was about to hurl. "That's nice, Ms. Edison."

"Call me Madeline, Winnie." Her voice was high-pitched, full of ups and downs, like a TV jingle. "I made Mason, my son, a pair of shoes just like these. He loves walking in the garden."

I nodded, but my brain wheels were churning. She had a son. No wedding ring. Three minus one equaled divorce. My dad was friends with a divorced woman?

"Mason's in school today," Dad informed me, as if I cared. Besides, what kind of kid goes to school on Saturday?

Madeline absently slipped her shoes on her hands and glanced from Dad to me. She reminded me of a nervous American Saddle Horse. "Mason's not in *school* school exactly. *Special* school . . . at the university."

I remembered there was a genius kid in Catman's class who took English or something at the university.

Madeline kept chattering. "I just hope he likes it there. He has trouble making friends. But he loves to learn. Most boys his age can be pretty rough."

Great. All we needed in town is another brainier-than-thou boy.

I pocketed the bag of carrots and tried to make my getaway. Maybe Dad hadn't known she'd drop by. But I hadn't seen a car outside, just Dad's cattle truck. What if Dad had driven to Loudonville and brought her here on purpose—to our house, without even asking Lizzy and me?

The umbrella popped open, knocking Dad on his backside.

"Jack, are you okay?" Madeline ran to his side.

I ran faster, easing in front of her. "You okay, Dad?"

"I'm fine." He got up and brushed himself off. He stood a few inches taller than Madeline, not quite as skinny, and was much better looking. My mom said Dad's curly, black hair was the first thing she'd noticed about him. "Look!" He pointed to the umbrella. "It works!"

I stared at the contraption, which hadn't opened like a normal umbrella. Instead, it stood upright on a flat handle. *That's* working?" I asked.

Dad fiddled with the top of the umbrella. "You put the camera here, and *voila!* It's a tripod!"

He pressed down on the top, shrinking the umbrella to a third of its height. Lifting the handle, he pulled down a black cloth cap and put it on his head. "Like this, it's an umbrella hat!" Dad paraded around, safe from unexpected kitchen rain showers.

He whipped off the umbrella hat and tugged on the cane handle. It grew long again and turned into a funny-looking golf club. "Perfect for practicing your swing while you wait for the commuter train." He took a practice swing that banged into the oven. Staring at the club, he muttered, "It would be easy to put a claw on this end, kind of a hand-extender. . . ."

"And he's adding a flashlight and a warning siren!" Madeline exclaimed. "I'm trying to get him to put in a radio."

I shook my head, as if the radio part were the only dumb idea here.

"I call it the Swiss-Army umbrella!" Dad announced.

He and Madeline leaned into the umbrella's handle, muttering something about installing flashing lights. Their heads touched.

Note to self: Two heads are not *better than one.*

I backed out of the kitchen.

My relationship with my dad reminded me of a Pinto mare Mom trained one summer. That mare had the roughest trot. It was the only time I'd seen Mom bounce in the saddle. But she'd said she didn't mind the rough ride, as long as the mare kept going forward.

Dad and I had been through some pretty rough ups and downs since Mom's death. The first year we hardly spoke to each other, leaving it up to Lizzy to keep us a family. Since we'd moved to Ashland, though, we'd both tried to keep the trot moving forward. But things kept getting in the way, making us back up again.

The night Madeline had called and I'd answered the phone, Dad and I had gotten into a huge argument. Our shouting match had ended with Dad declaring that he and Madeline Edison were just friends, as if that settled everything.

Friends. I felt like the only one on the planet who didn't have one.

That reminded me. *Hawk!* I'd stayed in the house too long. What if Hawk had come and I wasn't there? What if Catman couldn't hang on to her? I raced back through our junky yard toward the barn.

Catman waved at me, then pointed to the pasture.

There was Hawk, hands on hips, trying to get her horse to come to her.

"Hawk!" I cried. My regular voice is raspy and sounds hoarse all the time. But my throat had gone dry, so all I could get out was a squeak.

Hawk turned and said something to Catman.

The Appy flattened his ears, just like he had with Nickers.

"Towaco!" I screamed.

He bared his teeth and stretched his neck to take a chunk out of Victoria Hawkins.

Catman reached out a long arm and scooped Hawk away in the nick of time.

Applause burst from the other side of the fence. "Yea, Catman!" Lizzy cried. "You rock!" She and Geri cheered from a few feet away, which is as close as my sister will get to horses.

I scrambled over the paddock fence and ran out to them. "Way to go, Catman!" I could just imagine what Hawk's parents would have done if their precious daughter had come home with teeth marks.

"He tried to bite me!" Hawk narrowed her brown eyes at Towaco, who had already gone back to his droopy stance.

I couldn't believe the Appy would have gone through with it. But one thing was for sure: that horse was madder at Hawk than I'd imagined.

Hawk was wearing jeans, boots, and a fringed, suede jacket. Even in regular clothes, she manages to look like a model, or a Native American actress with her long, straight, black hair.

"I-I think Towaco was just kidding," I said, putting myself between Hawk and her horse.

Nickers had the good sense to stay away. "Your Appy is in a lousy mood today. I think he misses you."

Hawk wasn't about to be kidded out of it. "Towaco has never tried to bite me." As always, she pronounced each word precisely. She only slips into contractions when she's caught off guard, which is almost never.

"Forgive and forget, right?" I glanced at Catman for help.

"Have a groovy ride. Gotta split." He put Nelson down. "Promised I'd help Bart and Claire with Thanksgiving decorations."

Catman calls his parents by their first names only when they're not around. And they're the only ones who can get away with calling the Catman by his real name, Calvin. Calvin Coolidge.

"You decorate for Thanksgiving?" Hawk asked.

"Mr. and Mrs. Coolidge are big on lawn orna-ments," I explained, remembering the plastic figures that had covered their yard on Labor Day and Halloween.

"And they really dig Thanksgiving," Catman added.

"So do we!" Lizzy chimed in. She turned to Geri but talked loud enough for all of us to hear. "I'm baking Wyoming turkey, lizard potatoes, and frog Jell-O. Everybody in our family has to come up with three things they're thankful for—and you can't count family because that's too easy. And we all get to invite a friends to dinner if we want—although most of the time the friend can't really come because they're having Thanksgiving dinner with their families. But this year I invite *you!* And you can . . ."

Lizzy's voice trailed off, and my brain flashed me a full-blown picture of a Thanksgiving dinner at our Wyoming ranch. I was in first or second grade, sitting next to my mom, who had her hair in one long braid. She was smiling at Dad, and I think she must have been listing the three things she was thankful for. But my photographic memory never includes sound, so I couldn't remember what she'd said. What I could remember was that I'd had trouble narrowing my choices to three things I was thankful for.

What would I say this year? It would really be our first Thanksgiving dinner without my mom. We'd moved out of the ranch over Thanksgiving the first year. Last year I'd had the flu and spent the whole time in bed. Lizzy had gone to a friend's house, and I don't know what Dad did.

I hate *firsts* connected with Mom's death—actually, *first withouts*—first birthday without Mom, first Christmas without Mom, first Easter without Mom.

I knew Lizzy would make sure we kept the family tradition of naming three things we were thankful for. I wanted to do it too. But I didn't know what I'd name. Nickers, for sure. Who wouldn't be thankful for such an amazing horse? But where did I go after that? And who could *I* invite?

My only hope was Hawk. Riding with her seemed more important than ever.

3

$\mathcal{C}$atman strolled off, holding up the two-finger peace sign behind his back.

"I'll get your Appy ready, Hawk," I said, taking Towaco by the halter before Hawk could object. "Nickers and I will show you guys our secret hideout."

Towaco wouldn't lead for me, so I had to turn him in a circle to get him going. Mom used to say, "When in doubt, circle the horse."

It worked. Once he got his hooves moving, he let me take him to the cross-ties in the barn.

While I brushed her horse, Hawk sat on a bale of hay and stared at her boots. What she should have been doing was brushing her own horse. That's what Towaco needed. I love the Appy, but not like I love my own horse. Towaco needed Hawk.

"Want to ride bareback?" I asked, hoping she'd say yes. It would help her get in touch with her horse again.

"No," she answered. "I will ride Western. I do not trust that horse today." She fetched her heavy, Western saddle. Her dad had bought it for her the week before, even though she already had perfectly good Western and English saddles.

The leather creaked when we hoisted the deep brown saddle onto Towaco's back.

I slid the bridle on and handed the reins to Hawk. "I'll just put the hackamore on Nickers, and we can take off."

"Thank you, Winnie," she said. "This will be nice."

Nickers whinnied. She was as ready to ride as I was.

It took me two seconds to slip on the hackamore—a simple, no-bit bridle. "Let's take them out front," I called to Hawk, figuring Towaco might ride better if we got away from the pasture.

Nickers and I led the way through the barn and out to the yard.

I held the Appy while Hawk made a

smooth, perfect mount and settled into her new saddle.

I started to pray that Towaco would behave, but I stopped. My relationship with God was kind of like my relationship with Dad. After Mom died in the car accident, I stopped talking to God. Since we'd moved to Ashland, though, I'd started praying again—not like Lizzy does or my mom did. Lizzy prays about every little thing. I'd been concentrating on the big things, figuring God had enough on his mind not to have to hear about every little thing I worried about.

I swung up bareback on Nickers and scratched her withers. She pranced in place. "Okay, Hawk. Let's—"

"Winnie!" The front door slammed, and Dad trotted out of the house, followed by his *friend*. "Great! We caught you. I want you to show Madeline the barn before we leave to pick up Mason."

"We're going riding, Dad!"

Hawk was already urging Towaco to the street. The Appy acted tired, as if they were coming back from a ride instead of starting out. I didn't like to see Hawk using her heels to kick him, though, since kicking would only make him mad.

He responded better to leg pressure, and Hawk knew it.

"Let her go, Jack," Madeline said, standing behind him.

"This will just take a minute," Dad promised, leading Madeline to us. "Madeline is very interested in horses, aren't you, Madeline?"

Her back stiffened, a sure sign she was no horsewoman. "Well, I do wish I knew more about them."

Hawk got Towaco into the road and flicked him with the reins.

"Wait, Hawk!" I shouted. Beneath me, Nickers tensed, itching to follow them.

Hawk shouted back, "I have to keep him going while I can. He is acting like a plug! Catch up with us, Winnie!"

I glared down at my dad, hoping he'd read my mind and let me out of there.

"So tell Madeline about your problem-horse business, Winnie," Dad suggested as if I weren't staring bullets at him. "Show her the barn."

"I help horses with problems." I pointed to the barn behind us. "That's the barn." Turning back to Dad, I leaned down and whispered, "Dad, I have to catch up with Hawk."

"It's wonderful, what you're doing," Madeline said. "I wish Mason would ride. It would do him good."

I watched Hawk and Towaco amble farther down the road. Hawk had to kick and wave the reins to keep the Appy moving.

"Well, bring Mason over!" Dad insisted. "Winnie can take him for a ride anytime!"

"Dad, I fix problem horses, not problem people."

"Winnie!" Dad scolded.

"Winnie's right, Jack," Madeline agreed. "She might not know how to handle Mason."

Handle him? The kid must have been more spoiled than I imagined.

Dad wouldn't quit. "I insist! Winnie should take Mason for a ride."

Why couldn't he volunteer himself? He could use his Swiss-Army umbrella to take the kid's picture in the rain, while golfing at night and listening to the radio or something.

Nickers flicked her tail. I couldn't even see Hawk and Towaco anymore.

A fancy white car sped up the street, stopped in front of our house, and beeped the horn twice. Spider Spidell had another new car. The

Spidells own most of Ashland, including A-Mart, Pizza-Mart, Pet-Mart, and Stable-Mart, the fancy stable where Towaco had picked up bad habits from being kept in his stall almost 24 hours a day. Spidells care more about their cars than they do about their horses.

Dad crossed the lawn, and Mr. Spidell got out to meet him. The passenger door opened, and out came Summer Spidell, flipping her long, blonde hair over one shoulder. Summer is queen of the popular "herd" in my class. She has a way of making me feel like I got dressed in the dark.

Nickers snorted and backed away from them. My horse is a great judge of character.

"Willis!" shouted Spider Spidell, who got the nickname because his arms seem to reach all over Ashland. "Are my horse clippers repaired yet?"

Dad slapped his forehead. "Almost! I was working on them when I got this great idea for the perfect cereal bowl." He turned to Madeline. "You know how cereal always gets soggy? Well, I decided if you place a—"

"Willis!" barked Mr. Spidell. "I'm in a hurry. We're down to three clippers in the stable."

Dad nodded. Madeline and I moved closer, like accident gawkers on a highway.

Summer stared over at Madeline. Then she turned to me with a smirk that said, *So your dad does have a girlfriend.* Of all people, Summer Spidell had been the first person I know to actually see Madeline and Dad together.

I wanted to gallop Nickers right over her.

Note to self: Could one thing I'm thankful for be the fact that I'm not related to Summer Spidell?

"All right, Willis," Mr. Spidell was saying as he headed back to the car empty-handed. "But Monday at the latest, hear?"

Down the road came the pounding of hoofbeats.

I wheeled around to see Towaco trotting back. Hawk was hanging on to the saddle horn and bouncing all over her new saddle.

"Whoa!" she cried.

But Towaco paid no mind as he trotted across the ditch and up into the yard.

Hawk yanked the reins, and the Appy stopped a few feet from Nickers. "What is wrong with you?" Hawk screamed. "Winnie, this horse is now an official problem horse!"

I urged Nickers closer to Towaco. "He just

needs a fun ride, Hawk. Come on. You wanted to ride. We can go ride now. He'll be okay with Nickers—"

"Hi, Victoria!" Summer called in her sickly sweet voice. "What's wrong?"

"Towaco will not do anything right, Summer!" Hawk answered. "First he acts as if he can barely move. Then he races back in that awful trot."

"He misses you, Hawk," I insisted. "That's all! Let's just ride and—"

"You poor thing," Summer cooed. "I know! Why don't you come back to the stables with Daddy and me? You can ride one of our horses."

Hawk turned to Towaco. "That is not such a bad idea."

"Hawk?" I hated the whine in my voice . . . and the way it made Summer glow.

"I *am* sorry, Winnie. I am just not up to this today."

I took the reins and then watched as Summer and Hawk walked to the big, white car and drove off with Mr. Spidell.

"Well," Dad said, glancing from me to Madeline. "No problem. Right, Winnie? You can fix Towaco in no time." He laughed—a short, weak, weird laugh.

Madeline's lips moved in smile formation, but her eyes weren't in it.

A woodpecker tapped somewhere in the distance. On top of the barn a lone crow cawed.

"I-I've heard horses are highly unpredictable," Madeline stammered. "Probably why my Mason is so afraid of them."

"You didn't tell us Mason is afraid of horses." Dad looked almost hurt. "Well, you've come to the right place! Winnie the Horse Gentler can fix that! Right, honey?"

"What?" I swung my full attention to Dad.

"Tell Mason his worries are over!" Dad proclaimed to Madeline. "He's in good hands with Winnie the Horse Gentler! She'll get Mason over his fear in no time! Guaranteed."

"It's sweet of you to offer, Winnie . . . ," Madeline started, as if *I'd* offered, ". . . but I really couldn't impose—"

"Nonsense!" Dad broke in. "We *want* to help!" He smiled at me.

I'd rather have eaten worms than teach Madeline's brat to ride. But what could I say?

Madeline didn't say anything either.

"Good!" Dad exclaimed, as if we'd all agreed. "It's settled then."

I watched Dad and Madeline drive away in the truck. The gears cranked as Dad turned off our street.

Note to self: Score=Problem horse–1
Problem boy–1
Best friends–0

4

$\mathcal{A}$re you telling me there's nothing wrong with this horse?" Mrs. Hawkins spat the words in the vet's face.

I felt sorry for him.

I'd worked with Towaco all afternoon. It was getting dark when David Stutzman, the new vet, pulled in. Seconds later Hawk and her mom drove up behind him. The doc conducted a thorough exam of Towaco and pronounced that the Appy wasn't sick, which I knew all along.

"Temperature's normal. Blood count, CBC. Physically, the horse is fine." Doc Stutzman's Adam's apple jerked. He wiped his forehead, although the evening had turned cold.

I figured Doc was probably younger than my

dad. Short and stocky, he reminded me of a Manipur, a pony bred in India to carry heavy loads. His straight hair flopped across his forehead like a thick forelock. The doc looked ready to bolt from Mrs. Hawkins.

"What about his feet?" Mrs. Hawkins demanded. *Her* feet were encased in tall spike heels that kept sinking into the wet ground. "They're striped. And his nose! It's all splotchy, like measles or something."

"All Appaloosas have mottled muzzles and striped hooves," I explained, more to Hawk than her mom.

But truth was, I felt kind of betrayed by Hawk. She must have ridden with Summer and gone straight home to tell her parents how lousy Towaco had acted. I didn't get it. Hawk never talked that much to her mother in the first place. It didn't make sense that she'd tattle on her own horse.

Mrs. Hawkins had demanded that the vet examine Towaco immediately. And people do what she tells them to. She's a famous lawyer in our county, even more famous than Hawk's lawyer father.

I felt sorry for the Appy. Now, besides being

unhappy, he'd been poked, jabbed, and examined to pieces.

Towaco let out a sigh that turned into a groan, saying, *Nothing matters. I don't care what you do or don't do to me.*

"All right." Mrs. Hawkins flipped a lock of the Appy's mane. "He's losing his hair! Just look how thin that mane is. And the tail too!"

I didn't want to say anything to her. But nobody else was standing up for Towaco. "Appaloosa horses were prized for their thin manes and tails by tribes like the Nez Perce. Made it easier to run through brush."

"Well, *something's* wrong with him!" Mrs. Hawkins shook her finger at Towaco as she paced beside him.

I shut up for good. If Hawk's mom were a horse, I figured her for a spirited Hackney, the high-stepping horses driven in showrings. When they're coming at you, you better dive out of the way.

"He acts like an old nag. And I paid a pretty penny for that Appaloosa!" Mrs. Hawkins doesn't look much like her daughter, not at all Native American. Her brown hair was cut short, in layers that didn't move even when she shook her head.

Doc Stutzman backed toward his pickup. "There's one lab report I'll have to get in, but I don't expect—"

"Call me right away if anything shows up," she interrupted. "I'm leaving town Monday, early. I won't be back until after Thanksgiving. You can leave a message with my service."

Doc nodded and made his getaway.

I turned to Hawk. "You didn't tell me you were going away for Thanksgiving."

"I am not going," Hawk informed me. "Why would I want to go to some desert in Nevada with my parents? I will be staying with Summer."

"Oh." Hawk's mother stopped pacing. "That's the thing, Victoria. Summer's mother called my cell this morning. I've been meaning to talk to you. The Spidells are having company—her mother, the Boston Spidells, and the Oregon branch, too. They're all staying for Thanksgiving. It's just not a good time for you to stay with Summer."

"But Summer said—," Hawk started.

"Summer hadn't checked with her mother, Victoria. I'm sorry, darling."

Hawk tugged on a strand of her long, black hair. I don't think I'd ever seen her do that. "So what am I supposed to do?"

"You can stay here!" I blurted out. It was perfect. Hawk and I could ride together, go to school together, eat Thanksgiving dinner together!

Mrs. Hawkins glanced across the yard at my dad, who had a mouthful of nails and a handful of horse clippers. "It's all taken care of. There's a house-sitting service in Mansfield, highly recommended. They'll stay in our home and—"

"And *house-sit* me?" Hawk demanded. "No!"

"Well then . . ." Mrs. Hawkins looked cautiously around, across the junky yard and up to our house. ". . . maybe it isn't such a bad idea for you to stay here . . . if it's all right with Mr. Willis." She smiled at Dad, her eyebrows making question marks.

Dad, long nails sticking out of his closed lips, nodded.

"I'll be happy to pay you the going rate," Mrs. Hawkins hollered over to Dad.

Dad spit out the nails and coughed. "Nonsense! We'd love to have Hawk."

Yes! Lizzy can have Geri. And I'll have Hawk. Thanksgiving might actually be fun.

"See, Hawk? It's fine with Dad." I moved closer and scratched Towaco under his mane. "We'll have so much time to ride!"

Hawk smiled at me, her lips twitching. "That is really nice of you."

She leaned into her mom and whispered so I couldn't hear, but I did hear. "I don't want to stay here!" Then she smiled at me again.

Something rose in my throat, and I had to swallow it. I studied a Texas-shaped spot on Towaco's hip and wished I hadn't inherited my mom's great sense of hearing.

Mrs. Hawkins whispered back, louder than Hawk had, "You have two choices, Victoria: here or the house sitters."

Hawk didn't speak for what seemed like minutes while I ran my finger around Towaco's Texas spot. Finally she said to me, "I would love to stay. Thank you for inviting me."

If I hadn't heard the whispers, I actually would have believed her. One more thing Victoria Hawkins was good at—acting.

"Wonderful!" declared Mrs. Hawkins. "It's settled then. We'll call every day, darling."

Dad joined us. He was wearing a one-piece, orange work suit, with pencils, rulers, wires, and something green sticking out of the front pocket. "Want us to pick up your things now, Hawk?"

"No thanks," Hawk answered, too quickly.

"Why don't you settle in tomorrow?" Mrs. Hawkins suggested. "I'm sure you girls will have a lovely Thanksgiving!"

A lovely Thanksgiving?

Note to self: Don't count your turkeys before they hatch.

5

$\mathcal{D}$ad walked Hawk and her mom to the car,
but I stayed with Towaco. After they drove off,
I hung out in the barn for another hour. I rigged
a hay net from the ceiling of Towaco's stall,
trying to make eating more fun for him. Then I
dangled two plastic balls from the rafters and
tacked up a bright red stable blanket on the
wall.

All the while I tried not to think about what
I'd heard Hawk tell her mother. But the words
dangled in the air like the plastic balls: *"I don't
want to stay here!"* She'd been so upset, she'd
used a contraction.

"So what?" I reasoned with Nickers as I scattered fresh straw in her stall. "Could be a dozen
reasons Hawk said that. She's used to her own

43

room, for one thing. She knows she'll have to bunk with Lizzy and me here. Maybe she doesn't like Lizzy's cooking. I'll bet she's worried about putting us out. She knows we're not exactly rich."

Nickers rested her head on top of mine. I reached up and scratched her cheek until she sighed.

Note to self: You can fool all of the people some of the time and some of the people all of the time. But you can't fool a horse.

Sunday morning I hauled myself out of bed too late to eat breakfast. Lizzy had created green, frog-shaped pancakes. I don't know what she'd used to turn the batter green, but they smelled good, and my dad ate six of them.

Usually the Barkers swing by for us on their way to church. But since they were all in Texas, Dad drove the cattle truck and took up two spots in the church lot.

Lizzy ran off to sit with Geri and their friends, and Dad and I sat in the empty Barker pew.

When Hawk hadn't shown that morning, I'd

half hoped she'd meet us at church. It was a long shot since the Hawkins family didn't go to church. Still I couldn't stop myself from glancing back at the door, just in case.

Dad was doing the same thing.

"I don't think she'll come," I whispered.

Dad's eyes got huge. "You—well, she—I didn't exactly come right out and ask her, but—"

"*You* asked her to church?" I remembered that Dad had walked Hawk to the car. Maybe he'd asked her then.

"No." He glanced at the church door again. "Well, I did say if they didn't have a church home in Loudonville, they were welcome to—"

"Loudonville?" Then I got it. Dad wasn't talking about Hawk. He was talking about *her*. He probably expected Madeline Edison and her son to sit in *our* pew!

I slumped in the pew and folded my arms in front of me. "*I* was talking about Hawk, Dad!"

"Hawk?" He frowned, then faked a grin. "Ah . . . I see now. Um . . . no, no sign of Hawk."

The organ music started up, and Dad fumbled with his hymnbook.

I didn't sing. I barely noticed when Catman slid in beside me. I hardly heard the sermon. My

45

mind was buzzing, jumping from Hawk to Madeline to Towaco.

When I did tune in to Ralph Evans, our in-between pastor, he was talking about Thanksgiving. That made me think of the three things I'd have to claim I was thankful for at our Thanksgiving dinner. Then that brought me right back to Hawk, who'd be sitting at the table with us. And my thoughts would get away again.

Without realizing it, I'd made a paper fan out of my church bulletin, folding it back and forth in little strips. I tried to flatten it out again and noticed a bunch of Bible verses printed on the back. The last one grabbed my attention. When I looked away, I could still see the verse in my head. My mind had snapped a photo: *He delights in every detail of their lives. Psalm 37:23.* God had time for details? It made me think that it wouldn't be so bad to pray for little things.

God, sorry for not paying attention this morning. But I'm worried about Hawk. Would you mind making her have a great time at my house over Thanksgiving? And it would be great if you'd help me figure out what's up with Towaco, too. Plus, there's Madeline Edison—

"Winnie, are you coming?" Dad was standing

up. The church was nearly empty, and Catman and I were the only ones still sitting.

"We should get home," I said, scrambling over Catman. "Hawk might be waiting for us."

But Hawk wasn't waiting at our house.

Geri rode home with us and helped Lizzy make toasted peanut-butter-and-jelly sandwiches for Sunday dinner. As we munched sandwiches and barbequed potato chips, Lizzy and her friend talked reptiles and amphibians. Dad and I couldn't have gotten a word in edgewise, not that either of us tried.

"Don't you miss the bullfrogs?" Geri asked, not waiting for an answer. "I haven't heard one in over four months! They haven't been hibernating that long, just since early October. But they only sing late May to mid-July in Ohio. Don't you wonder why?" She took a bite of her sandwich. Grape jelly bubbled onto her plate. "I don't know if I can stand to wait until May!"

"I know exactly what you mean!" Lizzy exclaimed, passing the pea-and-bean salad. "Lizards hibernate even longer! Except Larry and his buddies, of course."

Larry was the first lizard my sister found in Ohio. Since then she'd gathered three others.

"My pet lizards won't hibernate, except for sleeping lots during the day." Lizzy flashed Dad a smile. "Thanks to my dad, the inventor. He built Larry that heated house."

Geri and Lizzy chattered about amphibians, bugs, and their classmates. I tried to picture Hawk at our table, eating grilled PB&Js and talking nonstop with me. I couldn't see it.

As soon as I could get away, I headed for the barn. Maybe it was a good thing Hawk hadn't arrived yet. It gave me more time to work on Towaco. If I could get the Appy back in shape, Hawk and I could ride every day during Thanksgiving break. We'd have to end up best friends.

I slipped the hackamore on Towaco in the pasture since he wouldn't come in for me. He didn't seem to care one way or the other. I jumped on him bareback and rode around the pasture. All he wanted to do was walk, so I guided him down to the pond and tried to get him to wade in.

The Appy just stood at the water's edge, not an ounce of curiosity in him. He didn't splash. He didn't even nuzzle the water. That worried me. Horses are born curious, but Towaco had no interest in anything.

Back in the pasture I had to work hard to get him to canter. When he did, he caught the wrong lead, wobbling with the outside leg stretching in front. I stopped and restarted him. It took three tries before he got it right, and then he stumbled and broke to a trot.

I'd imagined Hawk and me cantering through the pastures and exploring the back roads. But Hawk would never ride Towaco if he acted like this.

I scratched the Appy's neck and rode him back toward the barn. When I swung down from Towaco, my legs felt heavy. Usually I can ride all day and not be ready to quit, but now I felt worn down. I'd tried so hard to get Towaco to enjoy the ride that I hadn't enjoyed riding at all. It seemed to take forever to cool him down, but finally I did.

I missed my own horse. "Nickers!" I called.

Nickers whinnied from the back pasture. She tossed her head and took off at a dead gallop, thundering straight toward me. She didn't slow down until she was a horse's length away. Then she slammed on her brakes, skidding on her haunches to within inches.

"Show off!" I laughed and swung myself up

on her back, not bothering with the hackamore. Around us, the trees' barren branches swayed in the wind. I glanced at the gray, cloudy sky, wishing for snow, longing for the way it covers everything and evens out the world, making rutted ditches as pretty as gardens.

Grabbing a fistful of mane, I whispered, "Canter."

Nickers cantered from a standstill, her hooves barely touching earth. I took her in a big loop a second time, increasing pressure with my legs. Nickers sensed through my skin what I wanted, and she gave it to me, cantering the loop again and again.

"Whoa!"

She trotted, walked, then stopped.

"Good girl." I scratched her high on the withers, where she loves it. Then I decided what I needed, what we both needed, was a blind ride. Sometimes I like to give myself over to my horse, to try to sense what she wants in the same way she always senses my wants.

Wrapping my arms around her, I leaned my cheek against the crest of her neck, relaxed every muscle in my body, and closed my eyes, leaving her to decide where we'd go.

She whinnied low, saying, *Stick with me. You can trust me.*

I felt Nickers amble toward the pond. Then she changed her mind, trotted awhile in one direction, then another. Geese honked overhead. Leaves crunched underfoot. The distant smell of burned leaves swirled with the scent of acorns and horse.

Nickers broke into a canter, stretching it out, then circling and circling back. I lost my bearings, so I didn't know which end of the pasture we were in. But it was okay. Better than okay. Nickers and I were one, sailing across clouds in the middle of the sky.

I wondered if Towaco and Hawk would ever feel this way.

6

$\mathcal{N}$ickers slowed to a walk, then stopped.
I opened my eyes and sat up on her back.

There stood

Catman Coolidge in the paddock, holding
four cats. "Far out," he said. His wire-rimmed
glasses were pushed up on top of his head.

I slid off Nickers. "I needed a real ride after
Towaco. He's so unhappy, it's catching." The
Appaloosa hadn't budged from where I'd left
him.

"Let's split." Catman crooked his head, turned,
and walked off toward the barn.

"Catman! Where are you going?" I hollered.

He kept walking, into the barn and out of sight.

I kissed Nickers and ran after Catman, following just like his cats. Maybe Lizzy was right.

Catman Coolidge *was* the Pied Piper of Ashland, Ohio.

We hopped on our bikes and pedaled backwards out to the road. Catman had been the first person to buy a back bike. It was Dad's invention—a bicycle that goes forward when you pedal backwards. He even creates custom-made horns for each bike. Catman's horn sounds like cats meowing. Dad rigged mine to whinny, but I never use it. I get enough stares just pedaling backwards to school without whinnying.

I tried to keep up as Catman pedaled through a field. I bounced and dodged ruts and mud traps. He sped along as if we were biking on concrete.

"Where are we going?" I shouted.

"My pad," Catman answered.

A longhaired, white cat, eyes ringed in black like a mask, darted out. It just missed Catman's rear tire.

"Cool it, Burg!" Catman cried.

Cat Burglar is one of Catman's cats I know by name.

When we reached Coolidge Lane, we walked our bikes to his brownish lawn. Weeds are celebrated at the Coolidge estate. Dead leaves crunched under our feet and tires. The only mowed strip of lawn is in the front, where Mr. Coolidge sets up his lawn ornaments.

I dropped my bike and walked over to the lawn-ornament strip. A giant, plastic, brown oval, as tall as I am, sat next to an orange mound of something.

"What's that?" I asked.

"Thanksgiving," Catman explained.

"I don't get it." The closer I got, the more details came into focus. I could make out little bumps in the brown plastic, V-shaped arms on either side, and something like two bones sticking out behind.

"A turkey!" I cried. But it wasn't the gobble-gobble kind of turkey. This was the Thanksgiving-on-your-table kind of turkey. On either side of the roast beast, plastic drumsticks stuck out of the ground like bald, deformed trees.

"So what's the orange stuff?" I asked, poking the orange clumps. They felt like sponges.

"Sweet potatoes," Catman answered.

When we got to the front porch, the sound of the creaky, wooden steps flashed a photo to my brain—Coolidge Castle the first time I'd seen it. I'd thought it was deserted . . . and spooky.

Nothing much had changed—only the lawn ornaments. All three stories still needed paint, and the same windows were boarded up. But the house didn't seem spooky to me anymore or even weird.

Catman opened the door, and I stepped inside, along with half a dozen cats. As always, I got the feeling that I'd stepped out of a time machine into another century. Heavy red drapes hung over every window, matching the velvet sofas and love seats. The old-fashioned wood tables had claw feet. Instead of pictures, colorful tapestries hung on the walls.

Cats filtered in from every direction, prancing over the thick, Persian rugs, swarming at Catman's feet. I followed him to a closet at the end of a long hall. He opened the door.

At first I thought a fur coat was on the floor. Then it moved, and I made out Wilhemina, the fat orange tabby Catman had named after Charles Dickens' cat. Dickens had called his cat William until *she* surprised him with kittens. Catman's Wilhemina had the same idea. She was surrounded by so many tiny balls of fur I couldn't count them.

"They're so cute!" I whispered. My barn cat,

Nelson, had come from another of Wilhemina and Churchill's litters. Now he was a big brother. "Have you named them yet?"

Catman pointed as he listed off the names: "Hanson, Boudinot, Miffin, Lee, Hancock, Gorham, St. Clair, and Griffin."

"Where on earth did you dig up those names, Catman?" All of the Coolidge cats had unusual names, but he'd outdone himself this time.

"First Presidents of the United States," he explained.

I stared through his lenses and into his Siamese-blue eyes. "Wouldn't that mean they're all named George Washington?"

Catman shook his head. "Under the Articles of Confederation in 1781, eight men were elected president for a one-year term each. John Hanson was 'the first President of the United States in Congress Assembled.'"

Who knew? I learned more history from Catman's cats than I did from Mr. Stovall's social studies class.

"Can I use the phone?" I wanted to call home to see if Hawk had shown up yet.

The nearest phone was in the kitchen, but it wasn't easy to get to. The kitchen floor was an obstacle course of papers stacked in neat rows, forming a maze to the sink, with an offshoot to the phone. Each stack contained contest entry forms. I knew Catman's parents would fill out every entry and probably win quite a few contests.

I dialed and waited five rings before anyone answered and said, "Hello?"

I didn't recognize the voice.

"Is someone there?"

"I—It's—Winnie. Who's this?"

"Geri. Can I help you?" Lizzy's friend sounded like it was *her* home. She'd been spending enough time there. Lizzy said Geri's parents both work long shifts at the Archway Cookie factory.

"Is Hawk, *my* friend, there yet?" I asked.

"Nope. Sorry."

"Is my dad around?"

"Nope. Sorry."

"Lizzy?"

"Nope. Sorry."

I didn't know what else to say, so I said bye and hung up.

Catman was putting on the eight-track, the Coolidges' version of a CD player. I recognized

"Wild Thing" after two beats. I love that song. Wild Thing is what people used to call Nickers.

He looked up. "She there?"

Catman's almost scary, the way he just knows things. He'd known why I was calling home, and I didn't even think he knew Hawk was staying with us. I shook my head.

"Ring her at her pad," he suggested.

I shook my head again. What would I say if she answered? I didn't want to sound like I was begging. Besides, if she didn't want to come, I didn't want her.

But I did. "Catman, I don't know what to do with Hawk *or* Towaco. I've got to get that Appy turned around so—"

Before I could finish, the front door burst open, and Bart and Claire Coolidge danced in. I think they were doing the tango, cheek-to-cheek, gliding into the living room.

"Calvin! Winnie!" Mrs. Coolidge shouted, as if she hadn't seen us in decades. She was wearing a glittery red gown, skin tight, outlining three ridges above her waist. Her hair was piled at least a foot high and had green glitter all over it.

In his tux Mr. Coolidge looked like a penguin with a toupee. Around his neck he wore a Bugs

59

Bunny bow tie. "Sa-a-ay!" he shouted, not releasing his wife. "So a big Cadillac ran out of gas on Thanksgiving Day and pulled off the side of the road. Three compact cars stopped to help. Each car donated a gallon of gas from their own gas tank. What did the Cadillac say?"

I was already laughing. Bart Coolidge owns Smart Bart's Used Cars and has a million corny car jokes that make me laugh even when they're not funny. "I give up, Mr. Coolidge."

" 'Happy *Tanks*-giving!' Get it? Tanks . . . giving? I got a million of 'em!" He spun around, dipping his wife in a fancy dance maneuver.

She managed to twirl loose and spin my way. "What I wouldn't do for hair like this!" she exclaimed, sweeping my tangled hair off my shoulders. She shoved it on top of my head, eyeing me with the expertise of a hairdresser, which she is. "I could sculpt a masterpiece!"

I never know whether to thank her for liking my hair so much—especially since my sister is the one with great hair, and mine always looks like I've just breezed in from a runaway horse ride—or to take my hair and run. "You two look fancy," I said, trying to shift the conversation.

"We cleared the dance floor!" Mrs. Coolidge stood on tiptoes, like a ballerina.

I couldn't even imagine where they'd found a dance floor in Ashland. I pictured them tangoing through McDonald's or down the aisles of A-Mart.

"Mrs. Coolidge is quite the dancer." Mr. Coolidge winked at his wife.

She blushed, her cheeks turning as red as her dress. "Mr. Coolidge may look like a body-builder on the outside, but he's light on his feet."

Love must be blind. Bart Coolidge is Volkswagen-shaped, with a hairpiece on the roof.

"We better split to Pat's Pets," Catman said.

I wanted to go home and wait for Hawk, but I hadn't answered the horse-problem e-mails since Thursday.

"Good to see you, Mr. and Mrs. Coolidge," I called as we moved toward the door. "And . . . interesting Thanksgiving decorations."

"You should see what I'm putting up at Smart Bart's!" Mr. Coolidge challenged. "Sa-a-ay! Why did the turkey cross the road?"

Catman grabbed my wrist and whisked me out the door before I heard the punch line.

Maybe I should have stayed to hear it. Maybe

it would have helped me to laugh again at another corny joke, because the minute we got outside, I was hit by a wave of sadness. It came at me from all sides. I couldn't even say what I was sad about, but the feeling stuck to me like sweat.

Was this what Towaco felt like?

7

When Catman and I got to Pat's Pets, Pat was talking to a man and a kid. I watched them and tried to shake off the blanket of sadness I'd walked in with.

The boy struggled to hold onto a chubby puppy, whose tail wagged as fast as a horse's tail in fly season.

"I reckon it's a case of *puppy* love already! No offense." Pat chuckled, her apology aimed for the puppy. She never fails to excuse herself for her animal expressions. It's just part of the reason she's one of my favorite people. She reminds me of a feisty Shetland pony, good-natured but spunky and almost as short as I am. I don't think I've ever seen *her* in a bad mood. I wish my mom could have known Pat Haven.

Pat waved to Catman and me. Her brown curls bounced around her face, and she swiped one off her forehead as she turned back to her customers. "I'll make sure Eddy Barker stops by as soon as he gets home. If anybody can stop that puppy from chewing on furniture, it's Barker."

Besides working on the help line like Catman and I do, Barker has a part-time job helping Pat around the shop.

Catman and I settled in at the computer while Pat walked the new dog owners to the door. Barker had created the coolest Web site for the Pet Help Line, filled with all kinds of animal facts. People can even send in pictures of their pets, and Barker posts them.

All Catman and I had to do was answer the e-mails.

Pat came up behind us just as Catman logged on. "What should we do about the dog questions?" she asked.

Catman typed something fast, just using his pinkies and thumbs. Before I figured out what he was doing, I heard a phone ringing through the computer. The ringing stopped, and someone said, "Hello."

"Barker there?" Catman said into the computer.

Pat elbowed me. I had to admit I was pretty impressed.

Through the computer speaker, we heard somebody yell, "Eddy!"

Seconds later, Barker's voice came through. "Hello?"

Pat and I shouted our hellos to Barker. Then Catman read the dog e-mails to him. Barker answered each question as if he'd already thought them through ahead of time. And Catman typed in Barker's answers as fast as Barker gave them.

Catman read:

> My dog, Bruno, hates our mailman [actually a mail lady]. What can I do?

It was funny hearing Barker's voice and seeing his answer go up almost instantly on the screen:

> Bruno's just defending his territory and protecting you! In his mind, he believes barking makes the mail lady go away. He's done his job, and he's

proud of himself! Tomorrow, take Bruno out and introduce him to the mail lady. Show him you're all friends. Bring along some doggy treats for the mail lady to give Bruno.

When they finished the dog mail, we all shouted good-bye to Barker. Then Catman tackled his cat questions with the same speed he'd used on Barker's.

"Winnie, I hear tell you've got yourself company coming for Thanksgiving!" Pat exclaimed. "You and Hawk should have more fun than a barrel of monkeys! No offense."

"I hope so." That wave of sadness flowed through me again. "Hawk hasn't shown up yet though."

"Well, she's probably saying her good-byes. Can't be easy spending holidays without your folks."

I hadn't really thought about that. Maybe Pat was right. She usually is.

Pat wandered off to feed the tropical fish, so I watched Catman finish up the cat e-mails:

Dear Catman,

I get to buy a cat! Quick! Give me some tips!
—NewCat

Peace, NewCat!

1. Get your cat from a noisy family. 2. Make sure someone's loved your cat before it was 12 weeks old. 3. Check for clean, dry ears. 4. Choose a cat that digs moving objects. But hey, man! You're getting a cat! Any cat's cool! Bond, baby! That's where it's at.
—The Catman

Catman,

I am at my wit's end! My cat will not stop rubbing her face on me, even when I'm dressed for the office. How do I stop this annoying cat habit?
—Ms. N

Ms. N,

Thank your feline stars! Your cat thinks you're groovy. Cats have scent glands on their cheeks and chins.

Rubbing you with her scent marks you as her owner. Congratulations!
—The Catman

I was glad Catman didn't hang around to read over my shoulder. I can never come up with clever answers like he and Barker can. But at least I hope I'm helping the horses people write in about. I read my first e-mail:

Dear Winnie,
   My Paint horse won't trot! He paces or fox-trots instead. He's done this since he was born. What can I do?
—Frustrated

Dear Frustrated,
   The pace is a much smoother gait, right? If that's his natural gait, you won't have much luck changing him to a trot. Sure, it's unusual for a Paint to be a pacer. But can't you just enjoy that smooth gait?
—Winnie

I worked through each horse question and felt like I had decent answers. At the very end of the e-mails was a question about birds. We almost never got a bird e-mail.

> Can anybody tell me if birds can see colors? I want to decorate my zebra finch's cage, but my husband claims birds are color-blind.
> —Birdwoman

Hawk! I could call her at her house. And if she answered, I'd ask her the bird question. Then it wouldn't be like I was calling to beg her to come to my house.

I used the regular phone and dialed Hawk's number.

"Hello? Hawkinses' residence." It sounded like Hawk's mother.

"Um . . . I . . . is Hawk . . . I mean, Victoria, there?" I hate how I sound on the phone. My voice is gravelly all the time, but on the phone, it gets all shaky.

I heard Hawk's mother call her to the phone.

"Victoria Hawkins speaking." She sounded so formal I almost hung up.

"Um . . . Hawk? It's me. Winnie?"

I waited for her to tell me why she was still at her house. She didn't.

"Well, I'm at Pat's Pets. We got a bird e-mail, and . . . I thought you could help."

"Certainly. Will you read it?"

I read it to her.

Hawk didn't need much time to come up with an answer. "Tell her that birds do see in color. That is why they *are* colorful. Birds use color to attract mates or camouflage themselves. Zebra finches see more colors than humans. They are attracted by colors in the ultraviolet range, colors we humans cannot even see."

She stopped talking. The phone buzzed.

"Great answer!" I said. *Go ahead! Ask her why she's not at your house.*

"Is that all?" Hawk asked.

"Um . . . so I guess I'll see you . . . in a little bit? At my house?"

"My parents fly out in the morning. I can move my things over before school tomorrow . . . if that would be all right," she added.

When I hung up, the phone felt cold in my hand.

I told Pat and Catman bye and headed home alone, pushing my bike into a head wind that blew through me as if I were hollow.

8

$\mathcal{M}$onday when I headed out for barn chores, Dad was already outside working on the Spidells' horse clippers. I shivered in the morning chill, my breath making wintry puffs.

"Two down, one to go!" Dad shouted across the yard.

"You'll get it!" I shouted back.

He waved something that wasn't a clipper in the air. "Got tied up last night working on this. It's a dog watch!"

"Sounds good!" I hurried to the barn before Dad could ask me to test-drive the dog watch, whatever it was.

Towaco came in for oats, but he didn't devour it the way Nickers did. I mucked stalls, then ran back to clean up for school.

Lizzy was pulling something great-smelling out of the oven.

"Oatmeal pie!" Geri announced. Since Hawk hadn't come, Geri had slept over.

Lizzy blessed the pie, and we dug in.

I couldn't get in a word sideways as the three of us downed our oatmeal in pie form.

"What we want," Lizzy explained, taking a sip of fat-free milk, "is to show the world that lizards and frogs can be friends—"

"See," Geri chimed in, "we discovered that lizards love frog music! I used my frog CD!"

"—because," Lizzy continued, "if God's creatures, lizards and frogs, can learn to live together in peace, well, why can't we? It's a step toward world peace, Winnie!"

Great. Even lizards and frogs had friends.

They cleared the table, leaving Dad's plate and my grape juice and what was left of the pie.

"We're walking to school. Hawk can ride my back bike with you if you want," Lizzy offered.

"Thanks, Lizzy!"

They took off 45 minutes early. My little sister has always been the first one to school. I guess Geri would be the second.

I waited for Hawk and had another piece of

pie. Through the window I could see Dad fiddling with the watch. At his feet lay the clippers. I didn't want to be around when Mr. Spidell came for them.

A red sports car drove up. I ran outside just as Hawk and her dad were getting out.

Mr. Hawkins wore a dark gray suit, striped tie, and shiny shoes. His short brown hair had definitely been cut someplace other than Claire Coolidge's Beauty Salon. Even though he was a couple inches shorter than my dad, he stood up so straight he seemed taller.

Dad, in his old tan overalls, shouted, "Welcome!" He wiped his hands on his pant legs before shaking Mr. Hawkins's hand. "I'll help you carry things in." Dad opened the backseat door, and out flew a bright red bird with green-and-yellow wings. The parrot, a chattering lory, flew to Hawk's shoulder.

"Hey, Peter Lory!" I called. Hawk had named her bird after Peter Lorre, an actor who starred in the old gangster movies she likes to watch. "Hey, Hawk!"

"Squawk! Hey, Hawk!" Peter Lory cried.

"Thank you for having me," Hawk said, hugging a pillow to her chest.

"Thank you for coming," I said, sounding as weird as she did. The politeness reminded me how Dad and I were after Mom died—too polite, as if manners could make up for what we didn't feel anymore.

Her dad flashed a smile, showing perfect, white teeth. "Really, Willis. I appreciate this. Wish you'd let us pay you."

"For what?" Dad asked.

Mr. Hawkins laughed. Then Dad chuckled along. But I knew he'd really been stumped for a minute. Dad wouldn't dream of having somebody pay to sleep over.

The sports car was filled to the roof with stuff. I carried in a backpack and a down sleeping bag the first trip. I'd already told Hawk she could have my bed.

She and I carried in two more blankets, a CD player, a bag of makeup, her laptop, and a bunch of little stuff, while the dads hauled huge suitcases and a bunch of boxes. When we ran out of room in Lizzy's and my bedroom, we set things in our living room.

Finally Mr. Hawkins carried in a tall, gold birdcage with Hawk's two lovebirds on tiny perches. He set the cage down on one of the suitcases and frowned at the room, like he was leaving his daughter in prison. The birds stopped singing and scooted closer together.

Outside, a car tore up our street and squealed to a stop. We moved to the doorway in time to see Hawk's mom get out of a black Mercedes. She slammed the door and marched right for us. She wore a long, black wool coat with the collar turned up.

"You couldn't even wait for me?" she demanded, glaring past us to her husband. I wouldn't have wanted to be him. Then, as if she'd just noticed we were there, she smiled. "Hello, Winnie, Mr. Willis."

"Jack," my dad corrected, stepping back to let her in.

"Jack," she repeated. "We really appreciate this." She whispered something to Mr. Hawkins that didn't sound as nice as when she talked to Dad.

Mr. Hawkins shrugged. "You slept in. What was I supposed to do?"

Hawk stepped out of my room, her leather book bag over her shoulder.

"Victoria! There you are!" Mrs. Hawkins stepped over boxes to get to her daughter. "I wanted to drive you over myself, honey."

Hawk didn't say anything.

"Actually, it was a good thing I didn't come earlier," Mrs. Hawkins went on. "The vet called. He got the final lab report in. There's nothing physically wrong with the Appaloosa. The vet thinks it might be clinical depression. I didn't know horses could get that. Did you?"

Hawk glanced at me, obviously expecting me to step in.

"Horses get depressed," I said, my voice so hoarse Mr. Hawkins asked me to repeat it. I did.

"Don't they have drugs to help?" Mr. Hawkins asked.

"I was just getting to that," Mrs. Hawkins continued. "I asked the vet, and he said we could put Towaco on equine antidepressants."

"Don't do that!" I blurted out. They turned to me, and I was afraid nothing else would come out when I opened my mouth. "I-I can get Towaco to come around. *We* can . . . Hawk and me."

Mr. Hawkins put his hand on Hawk's shoulder. "Honey, if you want to sell your horse and get a new one, that's okay. I'll help you find the perfect horse."

"I have a client who raises show horses," Mrs.

Hawkins said quickly, putting her arm around Hawk too. "Would you like me to talk to him?"

I waited for Hawk to protest. I stared at her, but she wouldn't look at me. Instead she shrugged.

Could she possibly be thinking about it? Dumping Towaco for another horse? What is wrong with her?

Finally Hawk said, "I do not want to be late for school."

Mrs. Hawkins glanced at her wristwatch. "And we don't want to miss our flight."

"Lizzy left her bike for you, Hawk. We can ride together." I stuck my sack lunch in my pack.

Hawk glanced at her dad, then at her mom. "I think I will ride with my parents. But I will see you at school."

They offered me a ride, but I needed to bike to Pat's Pets after school.

I looked around at the boxes filled with Hawk's stuff and watched her parents fight over who got to drop her off. One thing was sure— Victoria Hawkins wouldn't have any trouble coming up with three things to be thankful for on Thanksgiving Day.

As I pedaled to school, backwards and alone,

I tried to convince myself that Hawk really would have biked with me if she hadn't wanted more time with her parents. Everywhere I looked, people were in twos—grown-ups jogging, kids walking to school. Even birds on telephone wires hung out in pairs.

By the time I got to Ashland Middle School, Hawk was already on the steps with Summer Spidell, Grant Baines, and the rest of the popular group. Grant's Quarter Horse was one of the first problem horses I trained. He and Hawk waved. But it was a "hello" wave, not a "come on over" wave.

The bell rang as I shoved my bike into the rack next to Catman's. No lock needed when you ride a backward bike.

I did giant steps down the hall and made it to Ms. Brumby's English class as the last bell stopped ringing. A legal non-tardy.

Ms. Brumby glared at me anyway as I headed for my seat. She reminds me of the Brumby horse. Brumbies are Roman-nosed, Australian scrub horses almost too disagreeable to train. Today she would have been a bay Brumby. She was dressed totally in brown, from her shoes to the tiny bow in her hair.

"Would *everyone* please take a seat?" she asked.

Since I was the only one not sitting, I slid into my seat next to Barker's empty chair. I missed Eddy Barker.

The class was noisier than usual, so Ms. Brumby raised her voice more than usual. "Class! It's not Thanksgiving vacation yet! However, anticipating your festive mood, I've come up with a special team assignment that should take us up to the break. I want you to pair off with a friend and prepare a report on friendship, in light of Tom Sawyer and Huck Finn."

All across the room, kids yelled, grabbing up partners left and right.

I tried to get Hawk's attention, but she and Summer sat in the back row and were already scooting their chairs closer together.

My chest tightened as I watched everybody else pair up. I'd have given anything to have Barker walk through the door. I looked for Sal, a.k.a. Salena. She's in Summer's group, but she's okay anyway. I spotted her by her hoop earrings, bigger than bracelets, and her bright orange hair. She'd already teamed up with Brian. They wouldn't get anything done.

"Kaylee!" I shouted to a Chinese-American girl I'd been wanting to get to know better. She waved, then shrugged and pointed to Amy.

"All right! Everyone have a partner?" Ms. Brumby shouted.

Please don't ask us to raise our hands if—

"Raise your hand if you don't have a partner!" Ms. Brumby demanded.

I faced front, stared at her brown shoes, and held my right elbow with my left hand. Could have been a hand raise, could have passed for an itch.

When I glanced up, our teacher was staring down at me. I peeked over my shoulder. No one else had a hand up.

"Hmm . . ." Ms. Brumby tapped her shoe. "Guess we have an odd number."

I knew who the odd number was.

We all did.

9

*M*s. Brumby frowned in concentration, still tapping her shoe. I pictured a Brumby mare pawing the ground. "I guess we'll have to make one group of three," she said at last. "Winnie, why don't you go join Summer and Victoria?"

Because I'd rather eat worms, that's why. I gathered my stuff and pushed through chairs to the back of the room.

Hawk pulled a chair from the row in front of her and turned it around for me.

"Two's company," Summer muttered, "and three's a—"

"Summer." Hawk stopped her from finishing. But Summer didn't need to finish.

"Well, this will be too hard with three of us," Summer whined.

Hawk took charge. "Did you both finish *The Adventures of Huckleberry Finn?*"

Ms. Brumby had taken two weeks on the works of Samuel Clemens, Mark Twain's real name. But we were supposed to finish reading *Huck Finn* on our own. I nodded. Once I got used to the way people talked in the book, I really liked it.

Summer sighed. "Are you kidding? If I have to listen to one more page of that dry, stupid book, I'll throw myself out the window!"

Note to self: Read a page of Huck Finn *to Summer. Several pages.*

"How should we start this thing?" Summer asked Hawk, looking right through me as if I were invisible. "I really need a good grade on this."

"We could list what we think makes up a friendship," Hawk suggested, looking back through me to Summer, "perhaps define what best friends are. Then we might compare the friendship of Tom Sawyer and Huckleberry Finn to . . ."

They wouldn't have noticed if I'd thrown myself out the window. Somehow, being invisible makes me feel worse than when Summer comes right out and says mean things to my face. At least then she's admitting I exist.

English class seemed to go on forever. I was relieved to get out of there and into life science class. The only class I really like is life science. Pat Haven has been our substitute teacher since day one of seventh grade. Our regular teacher left Ashland to "find himself," and nobody has heard from him since.

Pat was writing on the board: Symbiotic Relationship. When the bell rang, she dropped the chalk and turned around. She was wearing red tennis shoes, black slacks, and a red-checked shirt that made her look like a cowgirl. "I thought it would be fun to take our short week and look at animals in a different way."

No wonder I loved her class!

"Many animals form unique partnerships. Some of these partnerships work for both parties, and we call it a symbiotic relationship." Pat pointed to the chalkboard. "Other partnerships work well for only one of the partners, making that animal a parasite. You can do your report on any pair of critters you choose."

Kids groaned, but I thought it was a great idea. I knew I'd choose a horse for one of the animals in the partnership. I'd have to research to find the other partner though.

"So pair up with a partner, and . . ."

I didn't hear any of the instructions. Partners? I knew exactly where this was going. I was about to be odd man out again. My only hope was that we had an even number of kids in the class.

After a few minutes of chaos, the classroom settled into tidy sets of two . . . almost.

"Okeydokey!" Pat shouted. "All paired up? Did birds of a feather flock together? No offense!" She grinned at me.

I was the only one left in the front row. "Could I just do a report on my own?" I asked.

"Don't worry about it!" Pat exclaimed. "We'll get you paired off. Anybody need a partner?"

"Please," I whispered, biting my lip, praying she'd understand. "I want to do it by myself."

Pat raised one eyebrow. Then she nodded. "Alrighty!"

I breathed again.

She talked about the assignment, about partners and parasites. "Ideas anybody?"

"Maggots!" Brian shouted.

"Good one!" Pat agreed.

Hawk raised her hand. "Cuckoo birds?"

"Perfect!" Pat declared.

"That's my partner!" Summer chimed in.

"Hawk," Pat said, "tell us about that odd cuckoo-bird partnership."

"Cuckoos use foster parents," Hawk explained. "The female tosses out another bird's egg, say a warbler, when the mother leaves her nest. Then the cuckoo lays her own egg in that nest and flies away. The mother warbler hatches the cuckoo's egg. And even though the baby cuckoo pushes the rest of the warbler eggs out of the nest, the mother and father warblers work night and day to bring food to the ravenous cuckoo."

Hawk would love writing about birds. She already had an A report. Two more things for her Thanksgiving list.

After school Hawk said she'd see me later. She walked off toward Pizza-Mart with Summer, Grant, and Brian.

I biked to Pat's Pets as fast as I could. Catman was already there, finishing up his e-mails.

I answered three horse questions, then started researching horse partnerships on the Internet.

When I typed *horses* into the location bar, I got too many hits. I added *dependent,* and narrowed the possibilities to 23. One of the sites that came up was called "Horse Therapy." Under that was the heading "Hippotherapy."

As soon as I started reading about it, I knew I'd found what I needed: *"Hippotherapy is a specialty area of therapeutic horse riding that has been used to help patients with neurological disorders caused by stroke and head trauma. The patient is encouraged to form a partnership with the therapy horse."*

I thought about the summer in Wyoming when my mom had given lessons to handicapped kids. All I remembered was that two of them had wheelchairs. Somebody drove them from Laramie out to our ranch once a week. Mom knew just what to do to make the horses and kids partners.

"How'd you make out?" Pat asked as I printed out the pages on horse therapy.

I showed her all the good stuff about horses partnering with people.

"If that's not the cat's meow!" she exclaimed. "No offense!"

"I guess you have to be a trained therapist to

really do hippotherapy," I explained. "But lots of people who are good with horses do horse therapy. They get horses and handicapped kids to be partners."

The phone rang. Pat ran to answer it.

I waved good-bye and headed home. When I bounced my bike down the ditch and up into our yard, I could hear our phone ringing. I dropped the bike and raced inside to answer it, jumping over a huge vase of flowers sitting on the doorstep. I almost tripped over a package wedged in front of the door. I picked it up and ran for the phone. "Hello?"

Peter Lory flew to my shoulder, but I didn't see anyone else around.

"Is Victoria there?" came a voice through a noisy background.

"Mrs. Hawkins?" I guessed.

"Yes. Hello, Winnie. Could I speak with my daughter, please?"

I glanced around the house. "She's not back yet. Sorry."

Her sigh traveled all the way from the Nevada desert to my receiver. "Well, tell her to expect a surprise package from me tomorrow, will you?"

I still had the package under my arm. "I think it's already here."

"Are you sure? I don't see how."

I checked the label. "Yep. Says *Bob Hawkins* on the return address."

"Is that so?" She didn't sound pleased. "Well, that's not the one. Tell her *my* package should arrive tomorrow."

When we hung up, I brought in the flowers. A silver balloon flew above the vase with the greeting in pink: *Miss you!* The little card said it was from Hawk's dad. I wondered if Hawk had any idea how lucky she was to have two parents who were that crazy about her.

I set the flowers on the kitchen table and noticed a note from Lizzy: *I'm at Geri's. Tomatoes in the fridge. Lizard cookies on the counter.*

"Ring! Ring! Hello!" Peter Lory swooped through the living room, setting off the lovebirds so the house sounded like a jungle.

I thought I heard voices outside. Seconds later Hawk walked in and slung her book bag on the floor. "Hello, Winnie."

"Hello, Hawk." An awkward silence settled over us like a scratchy blanket. "Oh! Your mom called and said to expect a surprise package tomorrow. And your dad sent you flowers and a box."

"That's nice," Hawk said, crossing to the sink and getting a glass of water.

That's nice? "Aren't you going to open the package?"

She shrugged.

This was going nowhere. I'd never felt less like Hawk's friend. She reminded me of Towaco, not interested in anything.

I needed to ride Nickers. "Hawk, I'm going riding. You want to come?"

"Okay."

"Okay?" *Just like that?* I must have asked her a million times in the last two weeks.

Note to self: Don't look a gift horse in the mouth, no offense.

"Let's go then," I said. This was all Towaco needed, all Hawk needed, maybe all I needed.

"Let me change." Hawk headed for the bedroom. Unlike me, she didn't wear barn clothes to school.

She was still changing when Dad drove up and beeped his horn. I waved at him from the front step.

Hawk came out, and we started for the barn.

Dad honked again. He was still sitting in the truck. We waved and kept walking.

He honked and hollered, "Winnie, hurry!"

"Dad!" I shouted. "We're going riding!"

"We're going to be late!" he shouted back.

We stopped walking.

I shrugged at Hawk and trotted over to Dad. "Late for what?"

"For Madeline's! Remember? We decided you should meet Mason at their house before introducing him to the horses."

It sounded vaguely familiar, but I hadn't been paying much attention when they talked about it. I'd been too anxious to ditch them and go riding with Hawk . . . just like now. "I can't, Dad. Hawk and I—"

"You've known about this, Winnie. They're waiting for us. Get in the truck."

"Hawk's my guest! I can't just leave her and—"

Hawk interrupted me. "We can ride another time."

"Thanks for understanding, Hawk," Dad said. "I'm sorry about this. Why don't you come with us?"

"No thank you." She was already edging toward the house. "Towaco probably would not

have cooperated anyway. And I have home-
work."

"We'll have a late supper when we get back."
Dad revved the truck engine. "Help yourself to
anything you find, Hawk. Our home is your
home."

"It's not fair!" I protested.

"Get in, Winnie. Now." It had been a long
time since Dad had pulled out his mean voice.

I got in, slamming the door harder than I
needed to and sitting as close to it as I could.

I'd known it from the beginning, from the first
time I'd heard about Madeline Edison. *She* was
trouble. And nothing but trouble was going to
come out of that *friendship*.

10

Dad and I didn't speak until we were halfway to Loudonville. He gave in first. "I hope you're not going to keep this up at Madeline's. We want you and Mason to be friends."

We? As in Dad and Madeline? Dad, Madeline, and Mason? I thought of Hawk's cuckoo shoving the warbler egg right out of the nest.

Dad glanced over at me. "Don't make me sorry I brought you."

That's exactly what I wanted him to be—sorry he brought me. Sorry he'd brought *her* into our lives. My stomach knotted, and it was hard to breathe.

Neither of us said anything more until we hit Loudonville city limits. Then Dad sighed and white-knuckle gripped the steering wheel. "I want to tell you a little bit about Mason before we get there. He's—"

"I don't want to hear about Mason," I said, my voice low, sounding a hundred times calmer than I felt. Nothing he could say would make me want to be friends with the kid. *They* were the cuckoos. *I* was being shoved from their nest.

Dad turned up a street with look-alike houses too close together.

I stared out the window. One tiny lawn had a dozen cars on it, some up on concrete blocks instead of tires. "Can we please get home before dark?" I asked, not looking at Dad. "Maybe Hawk and I can still ride."

"I'll try. And I'm sorry I spoiled your ride, Winnie. But we did make these plans first."

We?

"There's a chance they'll want to drive over to the barn yet this evening, though," Dad explained. "Get things started . . . if things go well here."

Note to self: Do your part to make sure things do not go well here.

Dad pulled up under a leafless tree, and we got out of the truck. We walked up the short, cracked sidewalk to a wooden, A-frame house, smaller than our rental. The little front lawn had been plowed into dirt rows. Houses on both sides looked run-down, and the one across the street was deserted. Apparently, Madeline Edison's inventions weren't selling much better than my dad's.

"Welcome! Welcome to the Edisons'!" The weird, computerlike greeting roared down from the roof, which was covered in curvy antennae.

"It's automatic," Dad explained, pointing to a giant speaker. "A security system Madeline invented a few years ago. Announces everyone who steps onto their property."

I lagged behind him as he knocked at the yellow front door. The rest of the house had been freshly painted white. Peeking around to the side yard, I saw boxes of wires and metal gizmos scattered around. It looked like our yard, minus the appliance parts. No odd jobs, just inventions.

The door opened, and Madeline Edison grinned down at us. She wore a one-piece black work suit, kind of like Dad's, only with a belt. "You made it!"

We walked in, and I was hit with the same eerie feeling I get stepping into Coolidge Castle, only in reverse. Instead of leaping back in time, we'd jumped into the future. A silver net and tiny lights covered the whole ceiling, turning it into a starry sky. All the furniture matched, and it was all white. Except for one closed door at the far end, the whole house was right there in front of us, with only a partial divider to the kitchen.

"Thirsty?" Madeline asked. She took Dad's wrist and raised it to her nose. "The dog watch!"

I hadn't noticed the watch, so I checked it out, too. There was no dog on the watch. Plus the time was way off.

Dad's cheeks flushed. "Yep. Works perfectly. Advances seven times the normal rate, seven dog years per each human year."

Barker would have loved it, but I acted uninterested.

Dad followed Madeline to the kitchen "to help."

I couldn't stand to watch, so I plopped into the nearest chair. It felt weird, lighter than I'd expected, since it looked leathery. Rubbing my finger on the arm of the chair made me think of eyelid skin.

Dad came back and handed me a glass of un-asked-for lemonade.

"No thank you," I said politely. He made me take it. I started to set it on the coffee table. A tiny trapdoor flipped over, and a coaster appeared.

I wanted to go home.

Out the window I could see gray clouds. I wanted it to snow, but not until Hawk and I got our ride.

"Winnie?" Madeline called from the kitchen. "Will you turn on the lights out there, please?"

I searched for the switch in all the logical places, but came up empty. There were no lamps either.

Dad came up behind me. "Here." He walked to the door and used his chin to press what I'd thought was a door knocker. Light flooded the room. "Chin-lights! For when your hands are full." He demonstrated a couple of times.

Madeline walked in and set flowers next to my lemonade. A second trapdoor flipped open on the tabletop, offering her another coaster.

"Mason's in his room." She nodded toward the closed door.

"Why don't you go introduce yourself, Winnie?" Dad suggested.

I could have given him a hundred reasons. But I didn't particularly feel like hanging out with the inventors either. I crossed to the door and knocked.

"Just go on in!" Madeline called.

I opened the door and stepped into a room with nothing on the floor except a little boy. He sat cross-legged, staring up at his window. He couldn't have been older than six or seven, thin, with wispy, white-blond hair.

He turned and smiled at me without moving his eyes. He had a round face and wire glasses like Catman's, only with lenses so thick his blue eyes looked huge. I'm not sure what I'd expected, but it wasn't this.

"Hey." I stepped toward him, and his head swung back to the window. "I'm Winnie. You're Mason." I sounded like Tarzan with better grammar. "So you want to ride horses, huh?"

He didn't move. His body leaned to one side, as if off balance. The more I watched him, the more I could tell he was staring *at* the window, not through it.

Dad and Madeline walked in, and Madeline knelt by her son. "Honey, we have company." She smiled at us, not like she was apologizing for him or anything. "I told you about Winnie. And you already know Mr. Willis."

I glanced at Dad, wondering how well Mason knew *Mr. Willis*.

Madeline held Mason's head and gently turned it toward us. Mason turned it back, reaching tiny fingers toward the window.

"Mason." Madeline's voice stayed low and even. "Show Winnie your reading chair."

I scanned the room again. No chair. No bed. Nothing. Just a thick carpet on the floor and a bookcase built into one wall.

Madeline took Mason's hand and helped him reach what appeared to be twine dangling from the ceiling.

For the first time, I looked up. I was staring at the bottom of a bed. The furniture was all on the ceiling!

When Madeline pulled the twine, a big, white chair floated down. The chair matched the one in the living room. She slid something over one of the chair legs, and the chair stayed put. She did the same for a bed and another chair. I watched her, feeling like I'd walked into someone else's dream, where everything was light as air.

"Helium," Madeline explained. "Mason likes having his room uncluttered in the daytime. Right, Mason?"

The chair looked rock solid. But I knew the second the weight slid off, up . . . up . . . up it would sail. I thought about how wonderful it would be if everything worked that way, if the worries weighing me down could float away like that.

"Madeline's chair won first place at the Invention Convention," Dad said.

I knelt beside Mason, as the little light left outside fell across his face. His mouth turned up, as if he could burst into laughter any minute. "So, Mason, how old are you?"

He kept smiling out the window as if the best movie in the world were playing there. Then, without turning from the window, he stuck his hand out.

I wasn't sure if he meant it for me, but I shook his hand. His fingers felt like toothpicks, and his hand was so sticky it took a second for us to unstick.

"Sticky fingers!" Madeline laughed and kissed Mason's forehead. "You can wash your hands in the hall bathroom if you need to, Winnie."

Dad pointed down the hall. "Through there."

I hated that he knew where things were in this house.

The hall wall was covered with pictures of Mason, starting from when he was a baby. He was a cute little kid. There was obviously something wrong with him, and I felt lousy for not liking him before I met him. Dad should have warned me. Then I remembered he'd tried to talk about Mason in the truck, but I hadn't wanted to hear it.

Sorry, God, I prayed. *I still don't want us all to be friends, but none of it's because of Mason.*

Madeline was in some of the pictures, but none of the photos showed a dad. I had to admit that Madeline Edison wasn't ugly. She wasn't even funny-looking really, just tall. In every picture, Mason seemed to be staring at something off-camera.

I flipped on the bathroom light and shut the door. Birds started chirping, and the sound of rushing waterfalls filled the tiny, green bathroom. I flipped off the light, and the sound stopped. I turned on the light again, and the great outdoors returned. AstroTurf covered the floor and the walls and even the toilet. I washed my hands and got out of there.

In the living room, Madeline was helping Mason into his jacket.

"There you are! Shall we go meet us some horses?" Dad asked.

I nodded.

Any other time, I would have loved the idea of helping a kid like Mason over his fear of horses. Why did he have to be Madeline's kid?

11

$\mathcal{O}$nce out of the Edison house, I raced for the truck.

"Let's all go in my van!" Madeline shouted.

"Good idea," Dad agreed, although it couldn't have been a good idea. Now he'd have to come back with them just to pick up the truck.

I tried to get Dad's attention, but he was already lifting Mason into the green minivan.

Dad and Mason sat in back because the middle was too full of junk, and I rode shotgun with Madeline. She drove a lot faster than Dad. I figured if he hadn't been reading a rhyming book to Mason, he would have asked her to slow down.

"Mason likes you, Winnie," Madeline said

matter-of-factly, not like adults say to bigger kids when they want you to like their little kids.

"What's wrong with him?" I blurted out. Then, as soon as I'd said the words, I was sorry. "I didn't mean—"

"That's all right." She passed a car like it was standing still. "Some people call Mason *handi-capped*. I call him *handi-capable*. He has a lot going on inside of him. We're still working on getting it out. He's not always like he is today. He can say a few words. And we're both learning sign language."

She didn't seem to mind talking about it, so I asked, "Was he born . . . like this?"

She shook her head. "Head trauma . . . when he was just a baby."

Head trauma. My mind flashed me a picture. I tried to block it out, but I never can. I could see my mom's head against the steering wheel, blood trickling down her cheek. My mind had taken the photo seconds after the wreck that killed my mother.

I wanted to know more about Mason's head trauma, if he'd been in a wreck, too. But I wouldn't have wanted Madeline to ask me about Mom's accident. I changed the subject. "So where's Mason's dad?"

"Winnie!" Dad shouted up to us. I hadn't noticed he'd finished reading.

We'd turned onto our street. Madeline pulled up to the curb and got out to help Mason.

Dad rushed up to me. "Winnie, what did you say to Madeline?" he whispered.

"Nothing."

Light glowed from inside our house, and I saw Hawk sitting in Dad's chair, probably studying.

I led the way to the barn. Just smelling the hay and horse in my barn helped me get a grip on things again. This was my turf, the only place I felt really at home

Nickers came in from the pasture to greet me in her stall and nickered. She must have rolled in the mud. Dirt caked on her back and tangled her mane and tail.

"Is that your horse?" Madeline asked. "It looks so different from the other day."

"She just needs a good brushing." I led Nickers out to the stallway. "Come and meet Mason, Nickers."

Madeline stood behind Mason, her hands on his shoulders. Neither of them budged.

Dad took Mason's hand and led him over. "Come on, Mason. Winnie's great with horses."

Madeline trailed after them, her hands still on her son's shoulders, as if he were helium-filled and might float like his furniture.

Next to Nickers' stall, Towaco stood over his hay trough, not bothering to munch hay from it or from the hay net.

Mason turned and stared at Towaco the way he'd stared at the window, like there was nothing in the barn, in the world, except that horse. He started toward the Appy's stall.

"Not that horse!" Madeline shouted, directing him to Nickers. "This pretty white one." She held Mason's arm up so he touched Nickers' belly.

Nickers' skin twitched, the way it does when a fly lights.

Madeline jumped back, pulling Mason's hand away.

Nickers didn't like the sudden movement. She tossed her head and pawed the ground.

"Easy, girl," I cooed, wishing I could tell Madeline to take it easy.

"She's kind of touchy, isn't she?" Madeline asked, backing away.

"No." I answered too quickly. I tried again. "Not exactly. Arabians have thinner skin than most horses. But every horse has a muscle, the Panniculus, right under the surface of the skin. That's what makes their skin twitch for flies and dirt and stuff. It doesn't mean anything."

"You don't think she's too . . . spirited . . . too wild, maybe? Not for *you*, of course. But for Mason?"

"She's not wild," I muttered, thinking how people used to call my horse Wild Thing. She's spirited and sensitive. She reads moods, like Madeline's fear. But she's not wild.

"You haven't really given this a chance, Madeline," Dad said.

"You're right," Madeline admitted. "You're both right." She glanced around. "Mason?"

He'd moved to Towaco's stall and was staring at the Appaloosa. The Appy craned his neck around to stare back.

"Let's give this horse another try, Mason," Madeline said, picking him up and carrying him back to Nickers.

"It's really better if Mason walks up on his own," I suggested.

"I'm sure you're right, Winnie. It's just that

he's not used to horses." Still holding him, Madeline moved closer to Nickers.

Nickers danced in place as if the floor were hot.

Mason twisted in his mother's arms.

"What's the matter with Nickers?" Dad cried.

"Nothing's wrong with *Nickers*," I snapped. "She's just picking up on human fear."

"I know," Madeline said. "Mason's always been afraid of horses."

But it wasn't *his* fear I was worried about. I'm not even a horse, and I could feel Madeline's fear.

Mason squirmed and managed to slip through Madeline's long arms. His feet dropped to the floor. Madeline snatched him up again.

Nickers whinnied and jerked back on the cross-ties.

Madeline screamed.

Mason cried.

"That's it." She carried the crying, struggling Mason over by Dad. As soon as she did, Nickers settled down. "This was a mistake, Jack. I'm very grateful to both of you for trying, but—"

"Didn't the doctor say it would be good for

Mason to ride horses?" Dad reasoned. "You can't give up after one try, Madeline."

"I know it's my fault. I've never been good around horses," Madeline admitted.

Mason had been crying so loud I had trouble hearing anything else. Now he stopped crying so suddenly it was as if someone pressed an Off button. He was staring over his mother's shoulder at Towaco.

"Maybe we've had enough for one day," Dad suggested. "Let's go inside and talk about it calmly."

I stayed in the barn and finished grooming Nickers. She was as sweet as could be.

Later, when I walked into the house, Dad and Madeline were still talking about Nickers. Peter Lory sat on Madeline's shoulder. At least she wasn't afraid of birds. Lizzy and Hawk were sitting on the couch with Mason between them.

"His name is Larry," Lizzy said, stroking her lizard with her index finger.

"It's just that the white horse is so high-spirited, Jack," Madeline was saying. "Maybe I should find a pony, something more Mason's size."

"Ponies can be very high-spirited, Ms. Edison," Hawk explained. "Mason can ride Towaco.

Lately, my Appaloosa will not do anything but walk. He can be barnsour with *me* and trot back to the barn whether I am ready or not. But you can trust him."

"You can trust Nickers too." I knew my horse would be just fine with Mason if Madeline weren't there.

"Hawk's horse is that other one in the barn," Dad explained. "Mason did seem to like him."

"I don't know, Jack." Madeline Edison looked like she'd rather ride lions than horses. "Could Winnie work with that one?"

"Sure!" Dad exclaimed.

They still hadn't looked my way, even though I was all of five feet away from them. Maybe I really was invisible.

12

hat do you think, Mason?" Dad asked, squatting down by the couch to Mason-level. "Want to ride that pretty, spotted horse?"

Mason smiled, but his gaze went past Dad to our worn-out carpet. He scooted off the couch to touch an old carpet stain, staring at it as if it were the most wonderful thing in the world.

Dad stood up. "So we'll try again tomorrow! This time with Towaco?"

Madeline sighed and nodded.

Dad drove Madeline and Mason home after Lizzy fed us toasted tuna sandwiches.

"She seems nice," Hawk said after they'd gone.

"I like Madeline," Lizzy threw in, picking up plates and disappearing into the kitchen.

"You like everybody," I muttered.

Hawk yawned. "It is nice that your dad has a friend."

Something twisted inside me. "Dad doesn't need *her* for a friend! He has lots of friends." I imagined them together in the green van right then. I didn't like it. This whole Madeline-Dad thing was out of control, like a runaway horse.

"But, Winnie," Hawk reasoned, "your dad must get lonely sometimes. She seems like a nice friend. That is all I was saying."

A nice friend? Her? "You don't know her at all. Madeline Edison is . . . is . . ." I scrambled for something—anything. "She's . . . divorced! And I feel sorry for Mason."

Hawk got up from the couch. "I need to call Summer."

She was still on the phone when I got out of the bathtub.

We settled in for the night, Lizzy and Hawk in the beds and me on the floor between them. "I can sleep on the floor," Hawk offered for the tenth time.

"Honest, Hawk," I assured her, "I love your sleeping bag. Besides, even Peter Lory agrees this is the best spot." The bird had fluttered around the bedroom before selecting the foot of the sleeping bag as his bed.

When we'd all gotten quiet, Lizzy whispered, "Hawk, it's fun having you here. I love the flowers your parents sent. And doesn't Mason rock!" She rolled over onto her back. I couldn't see her, but I knew she'd still have her eyes open.

"So God, thanks for letting Hawk stay with us, and for making flowers smell like that, and for that little dimple in Mason's cheek when he looked at my lizard. Oh, and I love the webbed feet on Geri's favorite frog. And thanks for having Robert say hi to Alan so they're not mad at each other anymore. And it was super when—"

I glanced at Hawk, hoping she knew Lizzy well enough to know the prayers weren't for show. I've been eavesdropping on Lizzy's prayers my whole life, and I don't think anything of it when she switches over from talking to praying. But I didn't want Hawk to think it was weird.

Hawk stared at the ceiling, her hands behind her head. When Lizzy finished, Hawk turned on her CD. Soft night sounds filled the room, recorded crickets and dozens of birds. It reminded me of Madeline's bathroom, but I didn't say so.

After a few minutes Lizzy was making her little snoring sound. Hawk rolled on her side and looked down at me. "Winnie?"

I looked up. Pale moonlight flooded in through the window.

"Does Lizzy always pray like that?" Hawk whispered. "For every little thing?"

"I guess. Our mom prayed like that too." Sometimes Mom and I would be riding, and she'd shout to the clouds, "Thank you, God, for horses' manes!" Or "Thanks for the sound of hoofbeats!" Or "I love fetlocks!"

"Do you?" Hawk asked. "Do you pray for every little thing?"

I scooted deeper into the sleeping bag, fighting off the draft. "I have enough trouble remembering to pray for the big things," I admitted.

The verse from the church bulletin flashed into my head, complete with the gold bulletin and all the announcements: *He delights in every detail of their lives.*

"Does it work?" Hawk asked. "Praying for the big things?"

I thought about it. I'd prayed my mom wouldn't die. I'd prayed we wouldn't sell our ranch in Wyoming. I'd prayed Hawk would be my best friend.

On the other hand, I'd prayed we could stay in Ashland, and here we were. I'd prayed for a horse, and now I had the best horse in the world.

"Sometimes," I finally answered. "I mean, prayer probably *works* all the time. But you don't always get what you pray for." I knew I wasn't making sense. I wanted to wake up Lizzy so she could explain about Jesus and praying. Lizzy had kept praying just as hard after Mom died. It didn't bring Mom back, but I think praying helped Lizzy through it.

Hawk rolled over. "Good night, Winnie."

"Night, Hawk."

It took me a long time to get to sleep. It had been over two years since Mom died, and still, in the middle of the night I missed her so much I was afraid to close my eyes.

Tuesday morning in Ms. Brumby's class, Summer made prune faces while I tried to define *friendship* for our report. "I think a friend is somebody who, like, rides horses with you and—"

"Right!" Summer rolled her eyes. "And what if the horse bites the friend? And the *friend* can't fix the horse's problem?"

"Towaco didn't bite Hawk!" I protested.

Summer ignored me and turned to Hawk. "If you *don't* sell that horse, you need a bigger bit and a martingale to hold his head down. And my brother knows how you can tie a horse's mouth shut so he can't bite."

"Has he tried it on you?" I asked.

"Could we just do the report," Hawk pleaded. "Winnie has a good start. Friends do things together."

Summer leaned back in her chair and crossed her legs at the ankles. She wore six ankle bracelets. "Well, a *best* friend is someone who's *like* you." She sneered at me, making it clear I didn't qualify. To Summer Spidell, I'd always be the Mustang who didn't belong in her American Saddlebred herd.

By the time I got to life science, I couldn't wait to get going on my horse therapy paper. I pulled out the pages I'd printed at Pat's Pets. One story had a picture of a little kid, his legs in braces, smiling from the back of an Icelandic mare. Something about his smile reminded me of something . . . somebody . . . *Mason!*

Why hadn't I thought of it before? Horse therapy might work on Mason Edison. Dad said it was a doctor who'd suggested horse riding for Mason in the first place.

I read through all the horse therapy material again, this time with Mason in mind. Horses had helped thousands of people. A 13-year-old girl spoke for the first time after three weeks of riding lessons; she spoke to the horse! An eight-year-old boy had never responded to his mom. She'd tell him to brush his hair or get his shoes, and he'd keep staring out the window as if he hadn't heard her. After one month of horse therapy, the boy formed a partnership with a stable horse. The horse therapist could ask him to get a certain brush or even to saddle the horse, and the boy would do it. Pages and pages told how cerebral palsy kids improved their balance.

I have to tell Hawk about this!

I carried my notebook to the back row and plopped down next to Hawk.

Summer groaned. "What were we saying about *parasites?*"

Hawk laughed. Her lips tightened, and she seemed to try not to, but her eyes watered.

Parasites. One-sided friendships.

I didn't feel like telling Hawk about horse therapy anymore. I walked back to my own seat and waited for class to end.

I could smell the cafeteria before I walked in—a mixture of cabbage, cold cuts, and sweat. I took my place at Catman's table.

Across from me, M, one of Catman's friends and a guy of very few words, was dressed totally in black as usual. As far as I know, nobody's sure what the *M* stands for. He and Catman were nibbling sandwiches, which was odd because they can both down a whole sandwich in two bites.

A cackle came from Summer's table. Brian stood up and banged his fork on his plate, then sat down again.

"M wants to know how Towaco's doing," Catman said between nibbles. He'd eaten the crust off and kept turning the sandwich as he ate.

I hadn't heard M say a word, but I turned to him. He was nibbling like Catman.

"Thanks for asking, M. That Appy still isn't himself. But I have an idea." I told Catman and M about Mason and horse therapy. "So Mason and Towaco could end up partners. Might be what both of them need."

"Groovy." Catman held up what was left of his sandwich. He'd eaten it into a circle, with the insides gone, except for a line of sandwich down the middle and two small branches, the universal sign for peace.

M held up his sandwich, chewed to a perfect letter *M*.

"Talented," I said, wondering what it would feel like to have a friendship like those two.

"We're cutting out." Catman stood up, and so did M. "Later." And they were gone, leaving me at an empty table.

I still had Lizzy's cookies left, but I didn't feel like eating alone. Stuffing my garbage into my lunch bag, I headed for the trash can, which meant I had to pass Summer's table.

Nobody looked up until I got close. Then

Summer, her eyes fixed on mine, leaned side-ways and whispered something to Hawk. I heard the word *parasite,* and then Hawk burst out laughing.

I kept walking, past the trash can, past tables of noise and laughter, out of the cafeteria.

Who needs people friends, anyway? I told myself as I walked faster, my shoes echoing in the empty hall. *Not Winnie the Horse Gentler. She doesn't need anybody.*

13

$\mathcal{I}$ biked straight to Pat's Pets after school. I didn't want to give Hawk the chance to make up excuses for not coming with me.

As I logged onto the Pet Help Line, Pat came over to the computer. "Winnie, is Hawk with you?"

"No." I said it too quickly.

Pat raised her eyebrows. "You two gals not getting along?"

"Hawk's just staying with me because she doesn't have anyplace else to go. No big deal." I typed in my name and password and watched messages fill the screen.

"I reckon it's not easy on her, what with her folks away for the holidays," Pat suggested. "Did I tell you I'm chowing down with my sister's family in Cleveland for Thanksgiving?

Hawk won't let on, but she might be a bit homesick."

Hawk's parents were gone half the time anyway. And I knew for a fact she didn't get along with them very well when they *were* around. I wasn't about to let Pat make excuses for her.

Pat seemed to be waiting for me to say more. When I didn't, she left to help a customer.

I answered the four horse e-mails, taking extra time on the last one:

> Winnie,
>   I think my horse loves our goat more than she loves me! They share the same pasture and can't stand being apart. But I want to be my horse's best friend. What can I do?
> —Jealous

> Dear Jealous,
>   I understand. But you should be happy your horse has a good companion. As far as friendship goes, though, you're asking the wrong person.
> —Winnie

When I got home, Lizzy and Geri were in the kitchen. Geri reached into the fridge and tossed me a whole tomato, Lizzy's current favorite after-school snack. She'd picked up the habit from the Coolidges.

"Look what came for Hawk!" Lizzy held up a box with a leather coat in it. It smelled like a new saddle.

"That's from her mom," Geri said. "And this is from her dad!" Geri held up beaded leather moccasins.

Victoria Hawkins had it all.

Hawk walked out of the bedroom. "Hi, Winnie."

"Hi." I didn't even want to look at her. I could still hear Summer saying, *"Parasite,"* still hear Hawk's laugh. "I need to go get Towaco ready for Mason."

"Need any help?" she asked.

I started to say no, but I really did need help. All the horse therapy articles said you need three people to start out—one to lead, and two to walk beside the rider. I'd lead Towaco. Dad could be one of the walkers, but I sure didn't want Madeline to be the other one. I'd have asked Lizzy; but even though she loves spiders and lizards and bugs, she's scared of horses.

"I guess I could use another person to walk with Mason when they get here," I admitted.

Hawk followed me to the barn and helped me brush Towaco. We stayed on opposite sides of the cross-tied Appy, neither of us talking. I think we were both relieved when Dad drove up, with Madeline and Mason following in their van.

"We're out here, Dad!" I hollered.

Hawk stayed with Towaco while I walked out to meet them. Mason, in little cowboy boots and a riding helmet, came clomping toward me.

"Could I take Mason by himself for a while?" I asked. I shot up a prayer that Madeline would understand. "Hawk's helping, and we won't let him ride or anything until you guys come out. I just think he'll be less scared by himself."

"Without me freaking him out, right?" Madeline said it smiling. "Probably a good idea. I didn't think I was afraid of horses until I saw Mason with one."

She squatted Mason-level and fastened the helmet strap under his chin. "Honey, I want you to go with Winnie and see the spotted horse. Okay? I'll be there in a little bit." Her voice shook.

I took Mason's hand, and he walked with me, without even glancing back at his mother.

Hawk had Towaco saddled and the stirrups shortened already. I wanted to let Mason ride bareback, but I knew his mother couldn't handle it, not yet at least.

The minute Mason saw Towaco, he slipped his hand out of mine and walked straight to the Appy. He reached up to a spot on Towaco's shoulder, a white spot that looks like a tiny saddle.

"You like Towaco, don't you?" Hawk said, grinning, as if Mason's joy had rubbed off on her.

"It's okay to pet the Appy," I said.

Mason glanced at me over one shoulder, then turned back to Towaco and moved his little hand across the Appy's shoulder. The night before, I hadn't known if Mason understood us or not. Now I knew he did.

He touched another spot and stroked it. Then another and another, all across Towaco's belly.

Towaco's ears flicked. He craned his head around, the first real show of interest I'd seen in the Appy for days.

Mason moved up toward Towaco's head. Towaco pulled away and faced the wall.

"That's okay, Mason," I said. "Towaco's been in a bad mood lately."

But Mason wasn't about to give up. He

stepped around to Towaco's other side and reached for the Appy's cheek. Towaco turned away again. Mason followed him, crossing back to the left side of the horse. Back and forth they went.

"I am sorry, Mason," Hawk said. "I do not know what is wrong with Towaco."

Mason didn't stop though. He moved from one side to the other, following Towaco's head until Towaco gave up and let Mason pet him.

"Blow into his nostrils," I whispered, feeling the cold air charged with static electricity, as if the world waited to see what would happen. "His nose holes, blow into them. That's how horses say hello."

Mason stood on tiptoes and blew.

Nothing happened. Towaco didn't pull away, but he didn't blow back.

Mason blew again. And again.

"Maybe you can try it next time," I suggested.

But Mason hoisted himself up on his wobbly tiptoes and blew again.

Towaco's ears flicked, and he blew back.

Mason giggled and rubbed the Appy's muzzle.

My breath caught in my chest as I watched

them. "You don't give up, do you, guy? Blowing hello like that is a Native American custom, Mason. Hawk's Native American."

"I did not know the trick though," Hawk admitted.

Hawk watched over my shoulder as I showed Mason how to massage Towaco. "See how the Appy sways when you scratch his back? He's loving it, Mason!"

Towaco had been so out of it lately that he hadn't rolled in the dirt to get rid of the itchies. Scratching his back must have felt great. His eyelids drooped, and he sighed—horse language for *This is the life!*

Mason was still rubbing Towaco's back when Madeline and Dad joined us.

"Well, look at that!" Dad exclaimed. "Ready to ride, cowboy?"

"Everything all right, Mason?" Madeline asked.

"Mason, you want to ride Towaco?" I asked.

He turned to us, his smile so big he didn't need words.

"Here you go, Mason," I said, lifting him into the saddle while Hawk held the reins.

"Hold on to the horn, honey!" Madeline offered.

He took the saddle horn in both hands, and I guided his feet into the stirrups. Mason's body slanted to the right, throwing him off balance in the saddle. I tried to push him straight, but he tilted back, still angling to the right.

"Dad, you stand on this side and keep one hand on Mason's leg." I took the reins from Hawk. "You do the same on this side."

I led Towaco down the stallway. Mason laughed out loud. I walked the Appy past Madeline, to the end of the barn, turned, and walked him back.

"Are you okay, Mason?" Madeline asked as we passed her again.

You just had to take one look at Mason's smiling face to know he was more than okay. He giggled. He gurgled. He loved every minute, as I led him back and forth inside the barn.

Towaco changed too. He had spring in his step, and I sensed the Appy was finally enjoying something.

"I think Mason could do this for hours," I said as we made another lap of the barn.

"But I have a feeling this is about all Mason's mother can stand for one day," Dad whispered.

We ended the ride, and Mason helped us brush Towaco before I turned him out into the pasture.

Madeline thanked us, and Dad walked them to their van. Mason walked backward so he could stare at Towaco the whole way.

"See you tomorrow!" I shouted.

Just before he was lifted into the van, Mason turned and grinned, showing me the perfect dimple Lizzy had thanked God for the night before. How could I have missed it?

Wednesday was just a half day at school. About all the teachers managed to get from us were our papers. I'd stayed up late finishing my horse-partnership paper for Pat's class. Hawk had written the friendship paper on her own and turned it in to Ms. Brumby from the three of us.

By the time I got home after school, our house had been transformed into a zoo. Lizzy and Geri were baby-sitting their class pets over the holidays—a gerbil, two hamsters, and three white mice. Peter Lory swooped the room, flying circles above the rodent cages, while the lovebirds sang to each other. Willises' Wild World of Pets.

"Hawk called!" Lizzy shouted over the squawking and scratching. "She said she was eating over at Summer's tonight."

"But she can't!" I protested. "I need her to spot for Mason's ride. They'll be here any minute."

I could use a helping hand here, God, I prayed as I raced to the barn to tack up Towaco. I rounded the corner and rammed smack into Catman Coolidge. He didn't budge, but I fell backward.

Catman stuck out his hand. "Need a hand, man?"

Thank You, God.

As we got Towaco ready, I explained to Catman what I needed him to do for Mason's ride. We'd just finished saddling the Appy when I heard the van pull up.

Mason ran into the barn in his boots and helmet, a wool jacket buttoned up to his chin. He stumbled, and one leg dragged a little, but he didn't stop running until he reached Towaco.

Catman shook Mason's hand. "Nice threads, little man. Call me Catman."

"Today," I explained, "we'll take you for a spin in the paddock, Mason."

Madeline wrung her hands as Catman lifted Mason into the saddle. Dad and Catman took their positions on either side of Mason, and I led Towaco into the paddock. Madeline watched from outside the fence.

I grinned up at Mason. "Can you say 'Go, Towaco!'?"

Mason giggled. I tried the phrase again. He giggled again.

Madeline waved each time we walked by her. The sun was shining, taking the chill out of the air. It may have been my imagination, but it looked like Mason was already sitting up straighter, not so off balance.

After five trips around the paddock, Catman and Dad stopped holding on to Mason. They stayed close beside him but let him sit on his own. Mason never stopped smiling.

Dad hadn't said much. As we walked past the barn, circling again, he cleared his throat. "So . . . things are . . . okay?"

"Are you kidding?" I asked, smiling back at Mason. "Take a look at that face."

"And . . . everybody else? Getting along better? You . . . and Madeline?"

I glanced at Catman. He held up the two-finger peace sign. "I guess," I said.

"That's good. Because I . . . vite . . ." Dad mumbled the last part.

"What'd you say?" I asked. I looked to Catman again, but he stared off at the sky.

"Hmm?" Dad brushed something off Mason's boot. "Just that I invited Madeline to Thanksgiving din . . ." His voice trailed off, but not before I understood what he'd said.

I stopped cold. Towaco bumped into me. A stabbing pain started in my forehead and traveled through my skull.

My dad had invited another woman to Thanksgiving dinner!

14

Towaco shook his head, anxious to keep going. The air in the paddock had gone stale, sucked out by my dad's little announcement.

"Tell me you're kidding!" I shouted. "You can't invite *her!*"

"Shh-h-h!" Dad glanced at Madeline, who waved from the fence. "Don't you remember our tradition, Winnie?" He was trying to make his voice light, like this was nothing. But he couldn't look me in the eyes. "Each of us can invite a friend to—"

"A *friend?*" If I heard that word one more time, I'd scream.

Towaco tried to walk on. Mason squirmed in the saddle.

My throat ached, and my head throbbed. How

could he do this? And on Thanksgiving? Didn't he care about Lizzy and me? about Mom?

"We can talk about this later," Dad said. "Mason wants to keep riding."

"Is everything all right?" Madeline shouted from the fence.

Everything *wasn't* all right. It was all wrong. How could he have gotten over my mother that fast?

I turned Towaco back toward the barn. "We're done."

Catman took over, helping Mason down and unsaddling Towaco.

Without a word to anyone, I slipped the hackamore on Nickers and rode out of the barn and down the road. We followed a dirt path, galloping farther and farther from town. I tried to call up every mind photo of my mother. Usually I can't control which picture will flash back when, but one image flooded my mind.

It was the year Mom planned to cook our turkey overnight. Her friend said the meat would turn out extra juicy. Mom stuffed and basted a huge turkey and stuck it in the oven about midnight. When she woke up the next morning, she couldn't smell anything. That's when she realized she'd forgotten to turn on the oven.

I woke that morning to a loud noise coming from the kitchen. My mind picture had captured the scene as I walked into the kitchen. Mom had laughed so hard she'd dropped the turkey, then slipped on the greasy floor. When I saw her, she was sitting on the kitchen floor, a giant, raw turkey in her lap. And she was laughing so hard tears rolled down her cheeks. That was the year we'd eaten Thanksgiving macaroni. It was the best Thanksgiving of my life.

Thursday morning I tried to sleep in, but Hawk's lovebirds were singing, Peter Lory was squawking, and the gerbils wouldn't stop spinning their exerciser wheels.

"Happy Thanksgiving, Winnie!" Lizzy shouted. She was peeking into the oven. The scent of roast turkey floated out. I was grateful that Lizzy loved to cook. She says it brings out her creative side.

"Ditto," Geri said, stirring something in a big bowl.

"Thanks. You too." The last thing I felt like doing was celebrating Thanksgiving. But my sister was going to so much trouble, I didn't want to ruin the day for her. "Smells great, Lizzy."

"We're eating at three," she announced. "Dad's outside."

"Where's Hawk?" I asked.

"She went somewhere with Summer," Geri answered. "And her parents called twice to wish her Happy Thanksgiving."

Lizzy shut the oven and got out a bag of potatoes. "Dad said Madeline's bringing Mason over for another lesson this morning."

I cringed at the mention of *her* name. And with Hawk gone, Dad would have to help again.

Lizzy kept chattering. "Did you know they're coming for dinner? Geri can't stay because her parents won't let her. Her parents don't have to work. The whole cookie factory closes for Thanksgiving. Do you think Mason will like apple stuffing?"

I bundled up for chores and scurried out to the barn. Catman was sitting on a stack of hay bales, surrounded by cats. "Happy Turkey Day!" he called down.

"Glad you're here, Catman. I need you to spot for Mason again this morning."

"Right-on!" He leaped to the floor, got a brush, and moved into Towaco's stall. While I finished chores, Catman groomed and saddled Towaco.

I heard the van drive up. Then Dad and Madeline strolled into the barn side by side. I felt like hurling.

Mason walked straight to Towaco. As lousy as I felt, I couldn't help smiling at him as he hugged the Appy's neck and blew into his nostrils. Towaco returned the greeting. At least one thing was working out right.

Dad and I hadn't said a word to each other since Mason's ride yesterday. He greeted Catman and took his spot on the other side of Towaco.

Ignoring Madeline's "Happy Thanksgiving" greeting, I led Towaco out to the paddock.

Around and around the paddock we walked. Mason squealed, sometimes tilting his head back to laugh. He didn't need to be held to the saddle. Dad and Catman just tagged alongside.

Towaco nickered. His ears flicked back to listen to Mason, then forward to stay in touch with his surroundings. He hadn't been this alert in weeks. He and Mason had actually become partners, just like I'd read about in the horse therapy pages.

I tried to put Thanksgiving dinner out of my head. This ride was for Mason's sake, not Madeline's. "Can you say 'Go, Towaco!'?" I asked Mason. *"Go Towaco."*

We passed Madeline again. Dad waved at her over Towaco's back. My stomach turned. She waved back. I imagined both of them falling into a pile of manure.

Friends? What did he need with a woman friend? It should have been *my* mom there, waving, watching. My mom should have been eating Thanksgiving dinner with us. *Not* Madeline Edison.

From somewhere came the sound of girls laughing. Then Summer and Hawk appeared, running on the other side of the fence. I couldn't stop staring at them. In my head I could still hear them making fun of me: *parasite . . . parasite.*

They kept laughing, ignoring us.

All at once, Mason shouted, "Go, Towaco!"

Towaco broke into a trot. The rope slid through my fingers.

And I watched, stunned and helpless, as the Appaloosa ran off, out of the paddock, into the pasture, with Mason on his back.

15

I ran as fast as I could after Towaco. But the Appy trotted deeper into the pasture. Madeline screamed. Dad shouted. He tripped over something and fell.

I heard footsteps behind me, and Catman breezed past. He raced beside Towaco and grabbed the reins. "Whoa, cats!" he called.

Towaco stopped.

I caught up to them. "Mason, are you okay?"

Mason sat in the saddle laughing, one hand on the horn, the other hand petting the Appy. "Go, Towaco! Go, Towaco!" he shouted.

Catman and I stared at each other, then burst out laughing too. Relief rushed through me. Mason was fine, better than fine.

Thanks, God! I prayed, feeling it inside.

Dad limped over. "Is he okay?" He looked up and saw for himself. "Well, aren't you the cowboy, Mason!"

Madeline came trudging through the brush. Her long, gray coat was covered in burrs. Tears streaked her cheeks. She pushed past Dad and me and pulled Mason down from the saddle.

Mason started screaming.

"It's okay, honey," she said. "You're all right now."

Mason kicked, but Madeline held on. She glared at Dad. "You were laughing! He could have been killed, and you thought that was funny?"

"Mason was laughing," I explained. "I was trying to get him to say, 'Go, Towaco—' "

She wheeled on me, Mason still squirming in her arms. "Winnie, I expected more from you. He's just a little boy. Don't you understand? It could take him weeks, months, to get over this! How could you let this happen?"

I felt like the wind had been knocked out of me. She was right. Mason could have been hurt, and all because I hadn't been paying attention.

My mind had been on Hawk and Summer. "I'm sorry."

"Sorry isn't enough, Winnie, not when you're around Mason."

"Madeline," Dad said, "take it easy." Dad was sticking up for me?

She turned to Dad. "Take it easy? Is that all you have to say? Were *you* taking it *easy*? Is that why you weren't around when that horse ran off?"

"Come on, Madeline," Dad urged. "Be fair."

"All's cool that ends cool?" Catman suggested, keeping his distance.

Madeline glared at him. He held up the peace sign.

Mason squirted through his mother's arms, hit the ground, still crying, and tried to run back to Towaco. Madeline reached out long arms and grabbed him back.

"He just wants to pat the horse, Madeline," Dad reasoned. "He needs to—"

"He's seven years old!" she cried. "He doesn't know what he needs."

Dad shook his head. "You're too protective. Mason's getting a kick out of riding. You should be thankful—"

"Thankful?" she snapped.

"Yes, thankful! Winnie gave up her time to try to help. I think *thankful* is exactly the word I was looking for."

"Happy *Thanks*giving," Catman offered.

Madeline hugged Mason even harder. "We're going home, Mason."

"Maybe that's a good idea," Dad agreed, his voice prickly.

Madeline winced, just a little, but I saw it. "Fine," she said.

"Fine," Dad said.

She took off in one direction, and Dad in the other. Poor Mason, tears flooding his eyes, looked back at Towaco.

I should have felt happy to see Madeline Edison leave. It's what I'd wanted. But my hands were trembling, and the last thing I felt was happy.

Catman and I turned Towaco loose and walked back to the barn.

Hawk was waiting for us. "Was that your dad's friend I saw leaving? I thought they were staying for Thanksgiving dinner."

"What do you care?" I asked. I glanced around for Summer. If they hadn't walked by right when they did, if they hadn't been laugh-

ing, if they hadn't made fun of me in school
. . . none of this would have happened.

"Did I miss something?" Hawk asked.

"Ha!" It was all I could say. I walked past her
to the tack room.

"Bad scene, man," Catman explained.
"Towaco split with Mason on his back."

"How?" Hawk asked. "Winnie, you were leading Towaco, right? What happened?"

"*You* happened!" I screamed, storming up the
stallway at her. "You and Summer."

Hawk's face went blank. "What are you talking about?"

I knew I should stop right there, but I
couldn't. "You ran by, laughing, making fun of
who-knows-what, but probably me! I glanced
over at you and let go of Towaco!"

"So it is my fault?" Hawk asked, her voice as
cold as the north wind.

"If you'd been here helping me instead of
running off with Summer, none of this would
have happened! And if you *had* to be
gone, then you should have just stayed
away!"

Hawk took a step backward. "That is not a
problem!" She turned and stalked off, shouting

back words chipped from ice: "If my parents call, I will be at Summer's, for good!"

By noon the smell of turkey filled our house. I figured Dad hadn't told my sister about his fight with Madeline, since Lizzy made me set places for everybody at the table. I hadn't said anything about Hawk. So I set six places for three people.

Dad stuck his head in. "Any calls for me?" It was the fifth time he'd asked.

"Nope. Who are you expecting?" Lizzy asked. "What's up?" She glanced at me. I set out forks.

"Nothing," Dad said. "I just thought I heard the phone ring." The way he hung his head reminded me of Towaco when the Appy was so depressed.

I thought about how much Towaco had changed and wondered if Mason would ever get to ride him again.

I needed Nickers. "Back in a while, Lizzy." All I wanted to do was feel my horse . . . and soak up her warmth.

Nickers greeted me as if I'd been gone a week. I slipped into her stall and wrapped my arms around her neck, inhaling her, letting her winter fuzz tickle my cheek.

I sensed Catman before I glimpsed him in Towaco's stall. "Catman? I thought you'd be halfway through the Coolidge turkey by now."

He'd changed into his camouflage army coat and combat boots. "Big Thanksgiving sale at Smart Bart's Used Cars. We'll scarf turkey tonight." His piercing blue eyes could have been lasers. "You cool?"

"Me?" I ran my fingers through Nickers' mane. I'm lousy at faking things, and Catman is great at seeing through me anyway. "Catman, the last thing I wanted was for Madeline Edison to come to Thanksgiving dinner. It's still about the last thing I want. But I hate seeing my dad mope around like he lost his best friend."

Catman didn't say anything, so I went on. "Then there's Hawk. I don't even know if we're friends or not."

He sighed. "Bummer."

"I shouldn't have blown up at her, but it wasn't just because she and Summer ran by, Catman. Hawk's been rotten to me all week. It's almost like she's *trying* to push me away."

"I dig," he said.

"What do you mean?" I asked. "You think she *is?* Why would she try to drive me away?" Too many things were messed up. I couldn't think straight. I picked up Nickers' hoof, checked it, and set it down again. "I feel like I've single-handedly wrecked Thanksgiving."

"Fix it," Catman said.

"Oh sure! How? Call Madeline and beg her to come to dinner? Ride out after Hawk and drag her home?"

"Okay." He picked up a brush and started grooming Towaco. "I'll bridle. You call."

I watched him for a minute, his long arms sliding the brush down Towaco's neck, over his withers and back. "Thanks, Catman," I muttered.

I got the number from Loudonville information and dialed. *God,* I prayed, wishing I'd remembered to pray about all this stuff while it was happening, *please make this phone call work.*

Madeline answered on the first ring. "Hello?"

"This is Winnie." My voice sounded more hoarse than usual.

"Winnie? Oh, Winnie, I'm so glad you called. I owe you an apology."

"You do?" I'd half expected her to hang up on me.

"I never should have yelled at you like that. I'm so embarrassed. I just get crazy when I'm scared for Mason. You and that horse were great for him."

"I liked giving Mason rides on Towaco. So did Towaco. I'm just sorry I wasn't paying attention when the Appy took off. Is Mason okay?"

She sighed. "The only thing wrong with Mason is that he's angry with his mother for pulling him off that horse."

"You should bring him back," I said. "Today. And eat."

Note to self: In the history of Thanksgiving dinner invitations, there has never been a stupider one than this.

She didn't say anything.

I didn't want to like her. I still didn't want her to be part of our Thanksgiving. But she was Dad's friend. "Lizzy's fixed a ton of food. And Lizzy and Dad and I can't eat it all by ourselves."

"Does . . . does your father still want us to come?" She asked it so softly I could barely hear over Peter's chattering and the gerbil wheel and the lovebirds' cooing.

"Yeah, he wants you to come."

"Thanks, Winnie. We'll be there."

One down. But the hardest one was still to go.

16

By the time I got back to the barn, Catman had Towaco bridled. I slipped Nickers' hacka-more over her ears, and we led the horses outside. I jumped on my Arabian's back, and Catman handed me Towaco's reins.

I didn't know what to say to him. Catman had managed to show up every time I'd needed him. "Happy Thanksgiving, Catman."

"Right-on."

Leading Towaco behind me, I trotted Nickers toward Spidells'. As we got closer, I prayed, *God, I'm asking you for one of those detail things again. I need you to help me figure out what's going on with Hawk. Help me see through her the way Catman sees through me. I know you've got a lot going on today, so thanks for caring about this.*

I brought the horses down to a walk when we got to Spidells' long driveway. We passed Volvos, a Mercedes, a yellow BMW, two long black limos—fancy cars lining both sides of the drive.

A live band played, and well-dressed people clustered in groups across the lawn, under the warmth of big, open tents and flaming torches. At the edge of the yard, I spotted Hawk with Summer and Richard Spidell, Summer's big brother.

Summer was the first to turn around when I rode up. "What are you doing? Get those horses off the lawn! Can't you see we're having a party? For *people*?"

"Happy Thanksgiving to you too, Summer!" I said it just like Lizzy would have, only she would have meant it.

Richard's gray eyes narrowed, thin as his pencil-line lips. He's a junior in high school, almost six feet tall, but he still looks like an overgrown kid. "Winifred. Why aren't I surprised?"

"Because you knew I'd want to ride over and wish you Happy Thanksgiving in person?" I suggested.

"I'll be going now," Richard said, "in search of more suitable, mature company." He strutted off.

"Don't tell me," Summer said. "You want Victoria to ride with you. How *parasitic* of you. She's selling that problem horse anyway."

I turned to Hawk. "You're not, are you, Hawk? Not Towaco."

She shrugged, not looking at me.

"But you can't! Towaco's not just a horse! He's your friend! He's—!"

"No!" Hawk shouted so loud, heads turned. "Towaco and I *aren't* friends! We're not like you and Nickers. Maybe I wish we were, Winnie. But Towaco is not Nickers, and I am not you. It is not the same. Towaco and I . . . we . . . oh, I don't know what we are!"

"Hawk, you and Towaco are what you are. Can't you just enjoy your horse? Enjoy your friendship, even if it's not everything you think it should be?"

I stopped, hearing my words as if someone else were talking to me . . . about me. I'd been down on Hawk because our friendship wasn't like Lizzy and Geri's, or Catman and Barker's, or even Hawk and Summer's. I'd been so hung up on what a best friend was *supposed* to be like that I hadn't enjoyed the bits of friendship we did have—the little things, the details.

"Hawk, come and ride Towaco. You don't have to go home with me if you don't want to. Just enjoy your horse right now."

Towaco had been munching grass. He picked up his head and ambled over to Hawk.

"My mother will be waiting for us," Summer said, moving toward the house.

Towaco nuzzled Hawk. She scratched his chin, then looked from Summer to me . . . to Towaco. "Summer, tell your mother I have gone for a quick ride, please." She swung up on her horse.

I tossed her the reins, and we rode off, with Summer yelling after us.

I led the way to a clearing on the edge of town, and we both broke into a canter. We galloped up a dirt road, passed through an open field, and splashed through a creek, crunching ice crystals at the edge of the water. The wind bit my cheeks and made my eyes water.

Hawk didn't talk. It wasn't the ideal ride with a best friend, not like I'd imagined. But I chose to appreciate it, to be glad Hawk and Towaco were there, to enjoy the padded thud of our horses' hooves and the honking of geese overhead. I'd never thought of joy as something you choose, but that's what it felt like as we rode through the hills.

I breathed in the cold air, amazed by the purple clouds swirling through the sky, promising snow. I chose to enjoy the feel of Nickers' muscles carrying me so fast that the leafless trees blurred like tangles of crooked arms.

I glanced at Towaco and grinned at the little swish of his fetlocks. I remembered how much my mom had loved horse whiskers and velvet muzzles.

Before I even realized what I was doing, my heart was telling God thanks. It was as if I'd unlocked a door inside me, releasing a flood of thanksgiving—for fetlocks and purple clouds, for Hawk's friendship, whatever it was.

Then Hawk pulled Towaco to a dead halt.

I cantered Nickers back to them. "What's wrong?"

"I rode. Now I am going back to Summer's." Her face looked carved in stone.

"Hawk, what's going on? Look at Towaco! He's come out of his sadness or whatever it was.

So what about you? You have so much to be thankful for!"

A rabbit hopped behind Towaco. Two squirrels chased circles around a big oak tree. Hawk didn't seem to notice any of it. She kicked Towaco and trotted toward Summer's.

"Hawk?" I thought about just letting her go. Then I pictured Mason, staying with Towaco, walking from side to side until the Appy let him in.

"Come on, Nickers," I whispered. We overtook them easily. I pulled up right in front of the Appy.

Hawk sucked in her bottom lip. "You don't know anything," she said quietly.

She was right. I *didn't* know what was making her like this. *God, please help me understand.*

Things rushed into my head, details of the past week, little things I hadn't paid attention to because I'd been feeling sorry for myself. I thought about the look Hawk's mother gave her father when they dropped off Hawk. I remembered how they'd made it clear which present was from which parent.

"Hawk, where did your parents go?" They'd said Nevada, but I couldn't remember the specifics. I'd figured they were off on a romantic holiday.

Towaco stirred under Hawk. "Where?" Hawk repeated. "Reno. Ever hear of Reno, Winnie?"

I had heard of it. From TV or other kids. "Isn't that where people go to . . . to get a . . ." I let my voice trail off as everything came together.

"A *divorce!* Say it, Winnie! By this time tomorrow, my mother will be just like Madeline Edison."

I cringed, remembering what I'd said about Madeline being divorced. "I'm so sorry, Hawk."

"Don't be! Summer says she wishes *her* parents would get a divorce. She says most parents do sooner or later. And it works out just fine for the kids. Summer says they compete over you, let you do whatever you want, have anything you want."

I urged Nickers closer. She and Towaco blew into each other's nostrils, friends again. Towaco stretched his neck over Nickers' neck.

Then Hawk leaned onto the Appy's mane, wrapped her arms around his neck, and cried.

Nickers and I stayed beside them, totally still.

After a few minutes with no sound except Hawk's quiet sobs, she sat up and stared right at me. "I'm sorry, Winnie. I have behaved so horribly toward you." She stroked her horse's neck. "And toward Towaco. I never wanted to sell him. But I don't want to get too close—not to Towaco or to you."

"Why?"

She fixed her gaze on me. "Because it is easier that way. It doesn't hurt as much to lose things you are not close to. It's why I don't let myself have close friends."

"But you and Summer—"

"Summer and I will never be close. That's why we hang out. I have not told her how I really feel about the divorce. I couldn't get away with that around you. Summer and I have fun together, but that's it. That is how we both want it."

I couldn't believe how wrong I'd gotten everything.

Hawk wiped her eyes on the back of her sleeve. "But I do not want my parents to be divorced. My dad is moving out, Winnie. We might have to move. Nothing will ever be the same."

I knew what she meant. "You're right, Hawk. It won't be like it used to be, but you still have two people who love you. I know it won't be the same. Nothing has been the same for me since my mom died. But it hasn't all been sad, not all the time. There's been a lot of good too."

"Do you know why I didn't stay and help you with Mason yesterday or this morning?" Hawk asked. "I look at that little boy, with so many things he could be sad about, and I feel even worse."

"But, Hawk, Mason's the happiest person I know!" I struggled to get the thoughts and the words out. "Couldn't you almost see joy pouring out of him when he got near Towaco?"

She almost smiled.

"He loves that funny, saddle-shaped spot on Towaco's shoulder. And when Towaco sneezed once, I thought Mason would never stop laughing."

Now Hawk definitely smiled.

"Mason grabs onto the little things and doesn't let go. That's what I want to do. I don't want to miss all of God's little surprises because I'm tied in knots over something I can't change."

"I do not understand, Winnie. What surprises?"

"Like Peter's green-and-yellow wings, or Towaco's spots, or Nickers' nicker, or the way Lizzy snores . . ."

She laughed. She must have heard my sister too.

"Or Mason's dimples! Or friendship—with your horse or with another person, even if it isn't what you thought it would be. If we're so hung up on what it isn't, we lose what it is."

Hawk stared down at Towaco's shoulder. I wondered if she was looking for Mason's favorite spot.

A flock of geese flew over us. We looked up at the crooked *V* and listened to their honking. I prayed it would mean something to Hawk, that she could feel the joy I felt watching those geese.

"My mom loved geese," I said. "She used to say, 'God's in the details, Winnie.'" It had never made that much sense before, but now I understood at least a little of what she meant. *"He delights in every detail of their lives."* If I paid attention, God was everywhere. And so was joy.

We sat on our horses, Towaco's neck lopped over Nickers', until Hawk said, "I am starving. You think Lizzy has that turkey ready yet?"

17

$\mathcal{M}$adeline's van wasn't at our house when Hawk and I got back. We turned the horses out to pasture and headed inside the house.

Dad opened the door for us, letting out a surge of savory turkey smell. "I was wondering when you two would show up. Lizzy took the turkey out a while ago."

"We need to wait just a little longer," I said.

"Why?" Dad had black grease on his nose. Something about it made me want to laugh and cry at the same time.

"Because everybody's not here yet," I answered.

As if on cue, the minivan roared up our street and came to a squealing stop.

Dad glanced over my head to see outside. "But . . . how did . . . ?"

"I called Madeline," I confessed. "Don't get me wrong. I still don't think you should have invited her. And it feels weird to have her around, even if she's not as bad as I thought she was." How could I explain to Dad that it felt like betraying my mom to have another woman eat turkey with us?

Dad put his hand on my head. "Winnie, nobody could *ever* take your mom's place."

I looked up at him and rubbed the grease off his nose. He knew. My dad understood.

"Madeline and I are just friends," he said.

Hawk elbowed me. "Whatever that means. Right, Winnie?"

Mason pushed right past us and into the house, shouting, "Go, Towaco! Go, Towaco!"

Madeline walked in, wearing oven mitts and carrying a big bowl of sweet potatoes. Coils ran under the bowl, and a battery stuck out.

"I see you're trying out your new battery warmer," Dad said. "I was thinking that if you used a metal bowl, you might . . ."

We soon sat down to Lizzy's amazing Thanksgiving feast, Hawk on my left, Mason on my right. Lizzy said grace, which included not only the Wyoming turkey, lizard potatoes, warmed sweet potatoes, and frog Jell-O, but all the people seated around our table and just about everybody we'd met since moving to Ashland.

We talked about school and horse therapy and inventions while we ate. And when nobody could eat another bite of carrot pie, Dad explained our tradition of naming three things we were thankful for.

Madeline had to start. She named Mason (Dad forgot to explain the no-family rule), new friends, and electricity.

Hawk was next. "Towaco, the sound of a whippoorwill, and Winnie."

"Go, Towaco!" Mason cried.

We laughed. Then Lizzy named Jesus first; then Larry, her lizard; and Geri, her friend.

When it was my turn, I didn't know what to say—not because I couldn't think of anything. Twenty-four hours ago, I'd been afraid I couldn't come up with three things I was thankful for. Now I didn't know what to choose. "Nickers, Hawk, Mason . . . but I'm also thankful for the smell of hay, and the way light sneaks into the barn through tiny cracks, for fetlocks on Clydesdales, arched necks on American Saddle-breds, Arabian eyes, horse whiskers . . . and for Nelson, my barn cat. And Catman!" I wished Catman could have been right there so I could tell him I was thankful for our friendship, what-ever it was.

I'd been so sure I needed a *best friend.* I thought I knew what that was. But God was fill-ing that best-friend hole in his own way—with Catman and Hawk, with Mason and Nickers, with Lizzy and my dad . . . with himself.

My gaze fell on Mason. His face crinkled into a huge smile, and he pointed at the window. I turned and looked. "It's snowing!" I cried.

Hawk and I grabbed our coats and dashed to the barn for our first ride in the snow. We cantered bareback through fields, heading for Catman's to wish him a Happy Thanksgiving. Thick white flakes nearly blinded me, but Nickers knew the way.

The horses loved the snowfall as much as Hawk and I did. They kicked up their heels and whinnied back and forth through the snow.

God was in the details, and I talked with him: *Thank you, God, for the sound of horses' hooves, the*

caw of that crow, the swish of Nickers' tail, tree shad-
ows on fresh snow, Hawk's laugh. . . .

I could have gone on and on, listing so many
surprises. What I felt was more than happiness,
more than a feeling, as if God had reached right
past feelings to put his joy into the secret places
of my heart.

There were as many things to give thanks for
as there were snowflakes.

Hawk and I cantered onto the Coolidges'
almost-white lawn as Catman ran out, waving,
and a blanket of white wrapped up the world,
covering every bump in the frozen dirt, softening
edges, and bringing beauty to thistles and weeds.

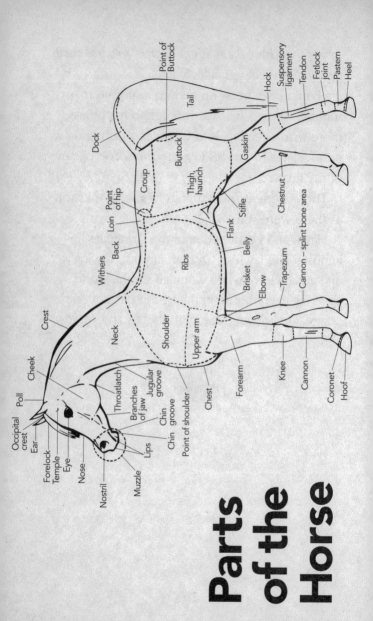

Parts
of the
Horse

🐎 Horse Talk!

Horses communicate with one another . . . and with us, if we learn to read their cues. Here are some of the main ways a horse talks:

Whinny—A loud, long horse call that can be heard from a half mile away. Horses often whinny back and forth.
Possible translations: *Is that you over there? Hello! I'm over here! See me? I heard you! What's going on?*

Neigh—To most horse people, a neigh is the same as a whinny. Some people call any vocalization from a horse a neigh.

Nicker—The friendliest horse greeting in the world. A nicker is a low sound made in the throat, sometimes rumbling. Horses use it as a warm greeting for another horse or a trusted person. A horse owner might hear a nicker at feeding time.
Possible translations: *Welcome back! Good to see you. I missed you. Hey there! Come on over. Got anything good to eat?*

Snort—This sounds like your snort, only much louder and more fluttering. It's a hard exhale, with the air being forced out through the nostrils.
Possible translations: Look out! Something's wrong out there! Yikes! What's that?

Blow—Usually one huge exhale, like a snort, but in a large burst of wind.
Possible translations: What's going on? Things aren't so bad. Such is life.

Squeal—This high-pitched cry that sounds a bit like a scream can be heard a hundred yards away.
Possible translations: Don't you dare! Stop it! I'm warning you! I've had it—I mean it! That hurts!

Grunts, groans, sighs, sniffs—Horses make a variety of sounds. Some grunts and groans mean nothing more than boredom. Others are natural outgrowths of exercise.

★★★★★

Horses also communicate without making a sound. You'll need to observe each horse and tune in to the individual translations, but here are some possible versions of nonverbal horse talk:

EARS

Flat back ears—When a horse pins back its ears, pay attention and beware! If the ears go back slightly, the horse may just be irritated. The closer the ears are pressed back to the skull, the angrier the horse.

Possible translations: *I don't like that buzzing fly. You're making me mad! I'm warning you! You try that, and I'll make you wish you hadn't!*

Pricked forward, stiff ears—Ears stiffly forward usually mean a horse is on the alert. Something ahead has captured its attention.

Possible translations: *What's that? Did you hear that? I want to know what that is! Forward ears may also say, I'm cool and proud of it!*

Relaxed, loosely forward ears—When a horse is content, listening to sounds all around, ears relax, tilting loosely forward.

Possible translations: *It's a fine day, not too bad at all. Nothin' new out here.*

Uneven ears—When a horse swivels one ear up and one ear back, it's just paying attention to the surroundings.

Possible translations: *Sigh. So, anything interesting going on yet?*

Stiff, twitching ears—If a horse twitches stiff ears, flicking them fast (in combination with overall body tension), be on guard! This horse may be terrified and ready to bolt.

Possible translations: *Yikes! I'm outta here! Run for the hills!*

Airplane ears—Ears lopped to the sides usually means the horse is bored or tired.
Possible translations: Nothing ever happens around here. So, what's next already? Bor-ing.

Droopy ears—When a horse's ears sag and droop to the sides, it may just be sleepy, or it might be in pain.
Possible translations: Yawn . . . I am so sleepy. I could sure use some shut-eye. I don't feel so good. It really hurts.

TAIL

Tail switches hard and fast—An intensely angry horse will switch its tail hard enough to hurt anyone foolhardy enough to stand within striking distance. The tail flies side to side and maybe up and down as well.
Possible translations: I've had it, I tell you! Enough is enough! Stand back and get out of my way!

Tail held high—A horse who holds its tail high may be proud to be a horse!
Possible translations: Get a load of me! Hey! Look how gorgeous I am! I'm so amazing that I just may hightail it out of here!

Clamped-down tail—Fear can make a horse clamp its tail to its rump.
Possible translations: I don't like this; it's scary. What are they going to do to me? Can't somebody help me?

Pointed tail swat—One sharp, well-aimed swat of the tail could mean something hurts there.
Possible translations: Ouch! That hurts! Got that pesky fly.

OTHER SIGNALS

Pay attention to other body language. Stamping a hoof may mean impatience or eagerness to get going. A rear hoof raised slightly off the ground might be a sign of irritation. The same hoof raised, but relaxed, may signal sleepiness. When a horse is angry, the muscles tense, back stiffens, and the eyes flash, showing extra white of the eyeballs. One anxious horse may balk, standing stone still and stiff legged. Another horse just as anxious may dance sideways or paw the ground. A horse in pain might swing its head backward toward the pain, toss its head, shiver, or try to rub or nibble the sore spot. Sick horses tend to lower their heads and look dull, listless, and unresponsive.

As you attempt to communicate with your horse and understand what he or she is saying, remember that different horses may use the same sound or signal, but mean different things. One horse may flatten her ears in anger, while another horse lays back his ears to listen to a rider. Each horse has his or her own language, and it's up to you to understand.

🐎 Horse-O-Pedia

American Saddlebred (or American Saddle Horse)—A showy breed of horse with five gaits (walk, trot, canter, and two extras). They are usually high-spirited, often high-strung; mainly seen in horse shows.

Andalusian—A breed of horse originating in Spain, strong and striking in appearance. They have been used in dressage, as parade horses, in the bullring, and even for herding cattle.

Appaloosa—Horse with mottled skin and a pattern of spots, such as a solid white or brown with oblong, dark spots behind the withers. They're usually good all-around horses.

Arabian—Believed to be the oldest breed or one of the oldest. Arabians are thought by many to be the most beautiful of all horses. They are characterized by a small head, large eyes, refined build, silky mane and tail, and often high spirits.

Barb—North African desert horse.

Bay—A horse with a mahogany or deep brown to reddish-brown color and a black mane and tail.

Blind-age—Without revealing age.

Brumby—A bony, Roman-nosed, Australian scrub horse, disagreeable and hard to train.

Buck—To thrust out the back legs, kicking off the ground.

Buckskin—Tan or grayish-yellow-colored horse with black mane and tail.

Canter—A rolling-gait with a three time pace slower than a gallop. The rhythm falls with the right hind foot, then the left hind and right fore simultaneously, then the left fore followed by a period of suspension when all feet are off the ground.

Cattle-pony stop—Sudden, sliding stop with drastically bent haunches and rear legs; the type of stop a cutting, or cowboy, horse might make to round up cattle.

Chestnut—A horse with a coat colored golden yellow to dark brown, sometimes the color of bays, but with same-color mane and tail.

Cloverleaf—The three-cornered racing pattern followed in many barrel races; so named because the circles around each barrel resemble the three petals on a clover leaf.

Clydesdale—A very large and heavy draft breed. Clydesdales have been used for many kinds of work, from towing barges along canals, to plowing fields, to hauling heavy loads in wagons.

Colic—A digestive disorder in horses, accompanied by severe abdominal pain.

Conformation—The overall structure of a horse; the way his parts fit together. Good conformation in a horse means that horse is solidly built, with straight legs and well-proportioned features.

Crop—A small whip sometimes used by riders.

Cross-ties—Two straps coming from opposite walls of the stallway. They hook onto a horse's halter for easier grooming.

Curb—A single-bar bit with a curve in the middle and shanks and a curb chain to provide leverage in a horse's mouth.

D ring—The D-shaped, metal ring on the side of a horse's halter.

Dutch Friesian—A stocky, large European breed of horses who have characteristically bushy manes.

English Riding—The style of riding English or Eastern or Saddle Seat, on a flat saddle that's lighter and leaner than a Western saddle. English riding is seen in three-gaited and five-gaited Saddle Horse classes in horse shows. In competition, the rider posts at the trot and wears a formal riding habit.

Gait—Set manner in which a horse moves. Horses have four natural gaits: the walk, the trot or jog, the canter or lope, and the gallop. Other gaits have been learned or are characteristic to certain breeds: pace, amble, slow gait, rack, running walk, etc.

Gelding—An altered male horse.

Hackamore—A bridle with no bit, often used for training Western horses.

Hackney—A high-stepping harness horse driven in showrings. Hackneys used to pull carriages in everyday life.

Halter—Basic device of straps or rope fitting around a horse's head and behind the ears. Halters are used to lead or tie up a horse.

Hay net—A net or open bag that can be filled with hay and hung in a stall. Hay nets provide an alternate method of feeding hay to horses.

Hippotherapy—A specialty area of therapeutic horse riding that has been used to help patients with neurological disorders, movement dysfunctions, and other disabilities. Hippotherapy is a medical treatment given by a specially trained physical therapist.

Horse Therapy—A form of treatment where the patient is encouraged to form a partnership with the therapy horse.

Hunter—A horse used primarily for hunt riding. Hunter is a type, not a distinct breed. Many hunters are bred in Ireland, Britain, and the U.S.

Leadrope—A rope with a hook on one end to attach to a horse's halter for leading or tying the horse.

Leads—The act of a horse galloping in such a way as to balance his body, leading with one side or the other. In a *right lead*, the right foreleg leaves the ground last and seems to reach out farther. In a *left lead,* the horse reaches out farther with the left foreleg, usually when galloping counterclockwise.

Lipizzaner—Strong, stately horse used in the famous Spanish Riding School of Vienna. Lipizzaners are born black and turn gray or white.

Lunge line (longe line)—A very long lead line or rope, used for exercising a horse from the ground. A hook at one end of the line is attached to the horse's halter, and the horse is encouraged to move in a circle around the handler.

Lusitano—Large, agile, noble breed of horse from Portugal. They're known as the mounts of bullfighters.

Manipur—A pony bred in Manipur, India. Descended from the wild Mongolian horse, the Manipur was the original polo pony.

Mare—Female horse.

Maremmano—A classical Greek warhorse descended from sixteenth-century Spain. It was the preferred mount of the Italian cowboy.

Martingale—A strap run from the girth, between a horse's forelegs, and up to the reins or noseband of the bridle. The martingale restricts a horse's head movements.

Morgan—A compact, solidly built breed of horse with muscular shoulders. Morgans are usually reliable, trustworthy horses.

Mustang—Originally, a small, hardy Spanish horse turned loose in the wilds. Mustangs still run wild in protected parts of the U.S. They are suspicious of humans, tough, hard to train, but quick and able horses.

Paddock—Fenced area near a stable or barn; smaller than a pasture. It's often used for training and working horses.

Paint—A spotted horse with Quarter Horse or Thoroughbred bloodlines. The American Paint Horse Association registers only those horses with Paint, Quarter Horse, or Thoroughbred registration papers.

Palomino—Cream-colored or golden horse with a silver or white mane and tail.

Palouse—Native American people who inhabited the Washington–Oregon area. They were hightly skilled in horse training and are credited with developing the Appaloosas.

Percheron—A heavy, hardy breed of horse with a good disposition. Percherons have been used as elegant draft horses, pulling royal coaches. They've also been good workhorses on farms. Thousands of Percherons from America served as warhorses during World War I.

Peruvian Paso—A smooth and steady horse with a weird gait that's kind of like swimming. *Paso* means "step"; the Peruvian Paso can step out at 16 MPH without giving the rider a bumpy ride.

Pinto—Spotted horse, brown and white or black and white. Refers only to color. The Pinto Horse Association registers any spotted horse or pony.

Post—A riding technique in English horsemanship. The

rider posts to a rising trot, lifting slightly out of the saddle and back down, in coordination with the horse's bounciest gait, the trot.

Przewalski—Perhaps the oldest breed of primitive horse. Also known as the Mongolian Wild Horse, the Przewalski Horse looks primitive, with a large head and a short, broad body.

Quarter Horse—A muscular "cowboy" horse reminiscent of the Old West. The Quarter Horse got its name from the fact that it can outrun other horses over the quarter mile. Quarter Horses are usually easygoing and good-natured.

Quirt—A short-handled rawhide whip sometimes used by riders.

Rear—To suddenly lift both front legs into the air and stand only on the back legs.

Roan—The color of a horse when white hairs mix with the basic coat of black, brown, chestnut, or gray.

Snaffle—A single bar bit, often jointed, or "broken" in the middle, with no shank. Snaffle bits are generally considered less punishing than curbed bits.

Sorrel—Used to describe a horse that's reddish (usually reddish-brown) in color.

Spur—A short metal spike or spiked wheel that straps

to the heel of a rider's boots. Spurs are used to urge the horse on faster.

Stallion—An unaltered male horse.

Standardbred—A breed of horse heavier than the Thoroughbred, but similar in type. Standardbreds have a calm temperament and are used in harness racing.

Surcingle—A type of cinch used to hold a saddle, blanket, or a pack to a horse. The surcingle looks like a wide belt.

Tack—Horse equipment (saddles, bridles, halters, etc.).

Tennessee Walker—A gaited horse, with a running walk—half walk and half trot. Tennessee Walking Horses are generally steady and reliable, very comfortable to ride.

Thoroughbred—The fastest breed of horse in the world, they are used as racing horses. Thoroughbreds are often high-strung.

Tie short—Tying the rope with little or no slack to prevent movement from the horse.

Trakehner—Strong, dependable, agile horse that can do it all—show, dressage, jump, harness.

Twitch—A device some horsemen use to make a horse go where it doesn't want to go. A rope noose loops around the upper lip. The loop is attached to what looks like a bat, and the bat is twisted, tightening the noose around the horse's muzzle until he gives in.

Welsh Cob—A breed of pony brought to the U.S. from the United Kingdom. Welsh Cobs are great all-around ponies.

Western Riding—The style of riding as cowboys of the Old West rode, as ranchers have ridden, with a traditional Western saddle, heavy, deep-seated, with a raised saddle horn. Trail riding and pleasure riding are generally Western; more relaxed than English riding.

Wind sucking—The bad, and often dangerous, habit of some stabled horses to chew on fence or stall wood and suck in air.

Author Talk

Dandi Daley Mackall grew up riding horses, taking her first solo bareback ride when she was three. Her best friends were Sugar, a Pinto; Misty, probably a Morgan; and Towaco, an Appaloosa, along with Ash Bill, a Quarter Horse; Rocket, a buckskin; Angel, the colt; Butch, anybody's guess; Lancer and Cindy, American Saddlebreds, and Moby, a white Quarter Horse. Dandi and husband, Joe; daughters, Jen and Katy; and son, Dan (when forced) enjoy riding Cheyenne, their Paint. Dandi has written books for all ages, including Little Blessings books. Her books (about 300 titles) have sold more than 3 million copies. She writes and rides from rural Ohio.

Winnie the Horse Gentler Series:

Collect all six books!

www.winniethehorsegentler.com

Get to know Winnie and Lizzy, plus
all of their friends, horses, and more at
winniethehorsegentler.com!

Check out all these fun features:

★ Post your own stories
   and photos of your pet

★ Trivia games

★ Articles by the author

★ Advice on pet care

★ And much more!